A Story of the Jinn Transcribed from the Actual Words of Amir Al-Braheem

BUDDY WORRELL

This is a work of fiction. All of the characters, names, incidents, organizations, and dialogue in this novel are either the products of the author's imagination or are used fictitiously.

Abbott Press books may be ordered through booksellers or by contacting:

Abbott Press
1663 Liberty Drive
Bloomington, IN 47403
www.abbottpress.com
Phone: 1 (866) 697-5310

ISBN: 978-1-4582-2300-5 (sc)
ISBN: 978-1-4582-2299-2 (hc)
ISBN: 978-1-4582-2298-5 (e)

Library of Congress Control Number: 2020920165

Print information available on the last page.

Abbott Press rev. date: 02/17/2021

This novel is dedicated to my grandchildren, Sydney and Andrew.

FOREWORD

Remember Me is a book you won't be able to put down. It is a thrilling story that begins in modern-day North Carolina and moves the reader back in time to the Crusades, all through the eyes of a young Englishman, William (Will) Wirral.

Will befriends a jinn, an ancient, immortal creature, and we follow their interwoven tales as they journey to the Holy Lands and back again. There are many close calls and narrow escapes, and the reader learns about life before electricity, motors and engines, and all the modern conveniences we take for granted. Imagine walking a year to reach a destination.

The reader learns about ancient culture, medicine, and food as well as about the various beliefs and religious practices of the time. This is an awesome journey through time and the reader is right there in the old monastery, the primitive village, the farm, the camp, and the battle.

Remember Me is fun and educational. Hooray for Buddy Worrell for the hours of research combined with a brilliant imagination.

Try it. I guarantee you'll like it.
Elsa Bonstein

PROLOGUE

Brunswick County, North Carolina, 2019

Dear Reader,

It doesn't matter who I am. You don't know me, and I choose to keep it that way. It's not that I am a hermit or curmudgeon or anyone you should fear. I just don't want my identity to influence these fantastic tales in any way! For now, you can call me "the Narrator."

You will need a little background on me to inform you how I ended up talking to an immortal creature from the beginning of time. I retired six months ago from a forty-year career in sales and marketing within the pharmaceutical industry. I did OK and made it to the vice president level. I lost my wife to cancer fifteen years ago and never remarried. We had no children, so I am now quite alone in this world.

Anyway, I was about one year away from regular retirement when a persistent and troubling cough sent me to my physician. She is an internal medicine specialist, so she inundated me with a long list of tests and scans. I think I already knew the outcome, but I was still shocked when her words registered in my brain. "Stage four, small-cell lung cancer. It is aggressive and has metastasized to your liver and colon."

I remember asking, "How long?

"Four to six months" came the answer. "Longer if we can shrink some of the tumors with radiation.

She suggested that I move up my retirement and live as hard as I could in the time I had left. You know, go to Hawaii or Tahiti or someplace like that. She could arrange the radiation treatments in most hospitals if they were not in the Third World.

So I retired a few months early but didn't go to Hawaii or Tahiti. I sold my condo in Philadelphia and found a small, oceanfront bungalow on the far east side of Ocean Isle Beach, North Carolina. It was surrounded by huge sandbags placed around the pilings in hopes the storm tides would not wash it away. Beach renourishment from last year had bought it some time, so I thought, *What the hell.* My real estate broker told me I was crazy.

"That place will be out to sea in less than a year!" she said matter-of-factly.

I remember answering, "Sounds about right!

My physician was as good as her word and set my radiation treatments up at New Hanover Regional Hospital about an hour away to Wilmington, North Carolina. The radiation seemed to help, and on days when I was not too wiped out, I would walk along the beach at low tide, picking up shells and talking to fishermen. This will come into play later in my story.

Several months ago, in early April, all the barrier islands in southern Brunswick County (Holden Beach, Ocean Isle, and Sunset Beach) experienced extraordinary tides—both high and low. I remember the high tide coming nearer and nearer to the sandbags surrounding my house and wondering if I or the house would ever be found after washing out to sea.

The following low tide revealed parts of the beach that were rarely dry, and as I walked along the newly uncovered sand, I spotted something shiny. As I got closer, I could see that the shiny object was an exposed corner of a partially buried box. I dug it out and found that it was about the size of a Black & Decker toaster oven. It was covered with a thin veneer of metal and showed no signs of corrosion from the saltwater. The box had a lid and was latched with a small clasp. Both the box and the lid bore inlaid markings of black and gold resembling ancient Egyptian hieroglyphs.

I wasted no time in walking back to my house to further examine my unearthed treasure. Once inside the house, I cleared my dining room table and set the box in the center. I was tempted to shake it once or twice but thought it better to open it gently and not disturb the contents, whatever they may be. A screwdriver and small set of pliers were all I needed to break the clasp and pry the lid off.

I fully expected to find a dank and ancient odor escaping from the box but, smelling nothing of note, went straight to examining the contents.

Neatly arranged and secured by velvetlike threads to the interior of the box was a yellow metal man's ring with a lightning bolt engraved on its face. If it was gold, it could be worth a few thousand bucks. The next item was a baseball cap bearing the *BB-55* and *USS North Carolina* logos from the Battleship Memorial in Wilmington. Nothing ancient about that! A small bundle of what appeared to be eagle feathers was next. I remembered that it was illegal to possess eagle feathers except those recognized for use in some Native American ceremonies. They were not fresh and had some kind of preservative on them. The next several items held no logic for me at all. A small vial of what looked to be blood, a golf tee, some shark's teeth, a toll booth token, several acorns, a crystal radio kit (I built one as a boy), and what appeared to be an authentic Spanish gold coin of the 1700s.

I stood in my dining room and scratched my head at the box and its contents.

It was on toward dinnertime and I prepared my evening meal of chicken noodle soup, saltines, and a protein shake. That was about all my cancer would allow. I always saved that double Jack Daniel's for bedtime to help me get to sleep.

It was still light outside and the April sunset was beautiful, but my walk earlier had left me exhausted so I lay down in the recliner, switched on the TV, and immediately passed out.

Hours later, I dreamed I heard a voice telling me to wake up. The voice also told me to put on the ring I had found in the treasure box.

"Third finger, left hand!" the voice ordered. My eyes fluttered momentarily but then relaxed.

"I said wake up!" the voice ordered in the tone of a command from one who is used to commanding. I remember that my eyes shot open and I scanned the room for possible intruders. Some of my exhaustion was gone. I slowly rose from the recliner to scan for burglars and then walked over to the box on my dining room table.

"You said put the ring on my left hand, third finger?" I asked aloud. My question was met with silence. "Are you sure only the left hand and third finger will do?" More silence. I felt quite ridiculous but proceeded to open the box, take out the ring, and place it on my left hand, third finger. The ring fit like it had been personally sized, even fitting over my edema-filled knuckles. I held out my hand to observe and admire the ring then, seeing a fleck of the box's interior stuck to the top of the ring, brushed it away with my other hand.

Instantaneously, the ring began to glow, red at first then refining into a blinding white. I was shaken up and terrified to the point of fainting but felt strength emanating from the ring. I became aware that a gentle warmth was spreading from my left hand, down my arm, and out to the rest of my frame. I also became aware that the walls of my home seemed to melt away, and I found myself on the beach and facing a man in a gray business suit with no shoes. He smiled at me, and I swear I saw large, white, shiny canine teeth before they disappeared.

"Who are you?" I stammered. "Better yet, what are you?"

"I am known by many names and have many faces. But you can call me Amir," the entity said. "I have a proposition for you that will benefit us both."

With a sudden blast of fortitude, I yelled at the man in the suit, *"Are you Satan coming to bargain for my immortal soul?"*

The man's expression changed to one of utter disdain as he roared, "Oh please! We haven't spoken to each other in ages!"

"Spoken to whom?" I shouted.

"Lucifer, of course!" the entity retorted, rolling his eyes, which began emitting sparks.

"Give me one reason why I should trust or even listen to anything you have to say," I challenged.

"Try this." He laughed and waved his arms at the tidewater beginning to surround my house. In an instant, the water receded, revealing one hundred feet of new beach in front of my bungalow. "Now shall we talk, or should I simply leave?"

And that is how I met Amir Al-Braheem, the last of the jinn.

Amir told me that the box was his and the contents were mementoes of stories he wanted told. He explained that he was an active participant in some stories, an enabler in others, and an observer in many. I asked him why he was so adamant that his stories be told, and he was vague at best. The closest thing to an answer I got was "I want to be remembered." He said that the "Most High," who he also referred to as "the Creator," had taught him that his destiny was to be in service to the sons of Adam—or mankind, if you will.

If this thing talks to God, who am I not to listen? I wondered.

It was like he read my thoughts because the next words from him were "Wise decision!"

He waved his arm again, and we were instantly back in my house. He said that he would return tomorrow evening to begin telling his first story for transcription. But before he vanished, I told him of my prognosis and that I may not live long enough to finish the works. His eyes flashed those sparks again, and that canine-filled grin reappeared.

"I am aware of your health and your prognosis, but hear me now. As long as you write for me, you will live. That is your part of the bargain. Now do you require anything else?"

"An old-fashioned cassette tape recorder and table mic would be nice. That way, I would be sure to capture all of your thoughts," I answered.

The machine materialized on my dining room table next to his box of treasures, and he vanished.

I remember standing next to my table for several minutes, trying to comprehend all that just transpired. My next thoughts were pangs of hunger, missing since the radiation treatments started. I also remembered that I had not coughed since opening his box. I went to the phone and called the number on one of the several magnets on my refrigerator. Sharkey's Pizza and Jack Daniel's on the rocks were sounding really good.

I distinctly remember wondering why this creature picked me to transcribe his tales. I would not find out until much later.

Dear reader, this is how the collection of stories came about, and yes, I am still alive and writing!

Sincerely,

The Narrator

One

Amir Al-Braheem, Commander of the Jinn
Jerusalem: The Ancient Walled City, 1095

> *Narrator's note: This was my first attempt to record and transcribe Amir's actual words. As he tells the story, his verb tenses and point of view may change.*

"My rage was not that of an intense fire. Over the years, it had become more subtle—somewhat like that of an ash-covered ember small and producing little heat and light—yet when disturbed was capable of reaching one thousand degrees," he began. "Evidently, it is possible to maintain this level of rage for over two thousand years. It is also possible to hate all in creation, as I did.

"According to legend, I and all of the jinn had been created by the Most High at the same time as the angels and mankind. The angels were created from light, mankind from clay, and the jinn from smokeless fire. I and my kind ruled the earth from the beginning, even as the angels ruled the heavens. I commanded the jinn as a supreme lord, taking tribute and delivering judgment for hundreds of thousands of years. Even my name meant *commander of the multitudes*. I had free will, unlike the angels, and could even question the Most High. The archangels—Gabriel, Michael, and Raphael—dared not do this.

"Early in the beginning, Luciel, the Morning Star, attempted to raise his mansions above those of the Most High in heaven. During the subsequent war, Luciel was cast out of heaven along with a number of allied angels and jinn. His name became *Lucifer*, and his legions were damned forever. I had no alliance with Lucifer and so remained neutral during the war. But the Most High was offended and gave dominion of all the earth to the recently created mankind and the sons of Adam, relegating the remaining jinn to a parallel existence. We could see mankind and the angels but could not interact with them or each other.

"Mankind would now have the Most High's attention and blessing. The jinn would suffer neglect, absence of purpose, and despair. We would be relegated to the realms of nightmares, bad luck, and noxious vapors. What had been pleasing in the sight of the Most High was now invisible. So went the legend!

"The reality was that next to the Creator, I was the most powerful creature in existence. I was neither pure good nor pure evil and actually regarded these labels as trivial. To the race of jinn, I was the commander. There was no demon I feared. No angel was my equal. I could command the elements of air, fire, water, and earth. I served no entity in the universe, and that, plus my arrogance toward the Creator, would be my undoing," he concluded before launching into the story.

"This story begins in the year 1095. I had been a powerless captive for over two thousand years—not that the passage of time was of much interest to me. My interest remained rage: pure, distilled, refined rage! Unlike some outcast angels, I did not scream or rant. After all, I was made of smokeless fire. My rage made me burn brightly but did not consume me.

"How do you describe a being such as me? In rare times, when I was visible to mankind, I was described as 'vaporous' from the ground to the waist but humanoid from my waist to head. This ratio of vapor to humanoid could change, as I (like all jinn) possessed shape-shifting abilities. I could take on the image of any object, animate or inanimate, with just a thought.

"Again, in rare times, when I wished to be visible to mankind, I was described as about twenty feet tall, depending on my trail of vapor. I was not clothed except for a wide belt, which separated my vaporous and humanoid sections. I was referred to as *he* but bore no male genitalia. However, my humanoid section (above my belt) was most definitely male. I was described as heavily muscled, almost barrel-chested. My head was bald, and the rest of me was totally hairless too. My face was oblong, with high, almost European cheekbones. My most prominent feature was my eyes. They were almond shaped and pupilless, blacker than any night sky, and flared with occasional rounds of sparks. If one asked my opinion of these features, I answered with one word." He paused, smiled, and said, "Magnificent!

"My situation at the time was not magnificent. Mankind and the jinn rarely interacted, but when they did, rumors of violence and destruction typically followed. Stories were told of humans being reduced to glowing cinders at the whim of a jinn. Pure poppycock! Mankind was terrified of these powerful creatures and prayed to the Most High to control the jinn and protect the sons of Adam from their seemingly omnipotent oppressors. The archangels agreed and begged the Most High to banish us from the earth or destroy us altogether. The Creator heard their prayers and fashioned a ring that possessed the power to control all of the jinn, including the ultimate jinn: me! The archangels asked for possession of the ring, but the Most High ordered it be delivered to the earth's greatest and wisest king: Solomon. Solomon was given power over all jinn by the Most High almost three thousand years ago.

"With the ring, Solomon could call all jinn to serve his palace court. I and all of the jinn were instantly subjugated. Most jinn rebelled at this. I, again, considered myself removed from the rebellion and refused to participate. But the ring from the Most High was all-powerful, and the jinn were transported to King Solomon's court for judgment, including me. For his judgment, King Solomon bound all of the remaining jinn in vessels or to a parallel existence. Their release from these vessels was totally dependent upon the Most High. They could be freed or cast out by his will only.

"But for me, a special punishment was allotted. I, Amir Al-Braheem, had served no one since the creation with the angels. I would grudgingly serve the Most High, but only to a point. I would not serve Lucifer, whom I considered weak. I would certainly not serve Solomon, who after all was a mere mortal. For this, Solomon, mortal but empowered by the Most High, bound me in a small box made of Palestine oak. Unlike the brass vessels in which he bound all the other jinn, this box was square, covered by a tight-fitting and sealed lid, and although it was small, it contained the phytochemicals necessary to bind even the most powerful jinn. Once relegated to the box of Palestine oak, I was captive. I could not speak, I could not escape, and I could barely interact. Even as an immortal, I became dead to the world.

"My prison was not that of a vault (as much as I wished it could be). The Palestine oak allowed sound to penetrate and created the maddening situation of hearing the outside world but not being able to respond or interact.

"Over two millennia, the box and I had been passed along, sold to traveling caravans and bartered as a magical object, but I had been unable to reveal my presence. My rage at this perceived injustice grew to the point of obsession, and I swore to myself that death would reward all and their seed who had wronged me. Swift and horrible death would be my response to any who dared interact with me. Given my release, I would take up the challenge of the Most High. But unlike Lucifer, I would succeed.

"Thoughts of escape, revenge, and death fed my rage and kept my smokeless fire intact. I did not need to eat as I drew sustenance from the atmosphere around me. In other days, I could travel great distances at great speeds, and I knew I would again. For the moment, I was simply a small, wooden box kept along with other supposed relics in the small cell of a Christian abbot, Father Joseph. The abbey was a small enclave near Jerusalem, surrounded by the Seljuk Turks and the armies of Islam. I had heard rumors of a war, but it was not my war. Let the Muslims and Christian crusaders kill each other. I bore allegiance to neither and given the opportunity would kill both."

Narrator's note: From here, the point of view shifts to others in the story.

Father Joseph knew nothing of his captive and angry prisoner. Father Joseph had been born near Damascus to Syrian Christian parents. They were devout in their faith and quite comfortable being surrounded by the followers of Islam. Young Joseph was fluent in Arabic, Hebrew, and Greek and showed great scholarly promise.

He loved to listen as travelers from faraway lands told stories of great cities, kings, and civilizations to the east. It was during this time of his life that he decided to study the ancient texts of Alexandria and Baghdad.

He craved the sciences introduced by Plato, Aristotle, Archimedes, and Pliny, now saved and entrusted to the Arabic scholars. Logic, geometry, architecture, and medical arts: all were written, copied, and preserved, just waiting to be rediscovered.

When Joseph was twelve, he was sponsored by a wealthy uncle to study at the Church of the Holy Sepulcher in Jerusalem. He delved into the old books of early Christianity and studied the arts and cultures found in the Old Testament. He especially was drawn to the book of Solomon and the multitude of manuscripts describing the wisdom and works of the Hebrew king.

In a very old and dusty volume, he discovered the legend of the jinn. To Joseph, it was fascinating fiction. No wondrous creature like this ever existed. There were no scholarly notes or treatises describing a being of fire. But it was a good story!

Father Joseph was accepted into the priesthood but sought no parish. He preferred the cloistered existence of an abbey where he could concentrate on his readings and translations. Up until the fall of Palestine to the Seljuk Turks, Christians were well treated and interacted freely with the local population and the maze of caravan travelers. Now there was a prevalent ill feeing toward all "infidels" as other religions were referred. Some shrines had been destroyed and Christians denied access to their churches.

Merchants had brought word that Pope Urban II was calling for an army of crusaders to come and free the Holy Land from the Saracen (as most Arabs were called). Father Joseph could only retreat to his abbey, work with his manuscripts, translations, and holy relics, and pray that a war was not inevitable.

One of those relics was a one-inch square box made of Palestine oak. Father Joseph had bartered it from an Arab trader while on a visit to the ancient site of Solomon's temple. The trader had made vociferous claims of magic and fiery powers contained within. He pronounced that it came with multiple curses to anyone who opened it, even unto death!

Father Joseph could see that to break the seal on the lid would destroy the box. "A small silver coin was a pittance for such a relic!" the trader cried. It was interesting, and Father Joseph knew that some ancients had attributed magical powers to vessels made of this material, so he gave the trader a small silver coin and took possession of the box.

Amir could see and hear the transaction, and it flamed his rage again. He was purchased for earthly metal? But no noise came from the box. No tremor or vibration emerged when Father Joseph took the box in his hand. A slight sensation of heat was the only oddity of the box, and Father Joseph dismissed that as resulting from the desert sun.

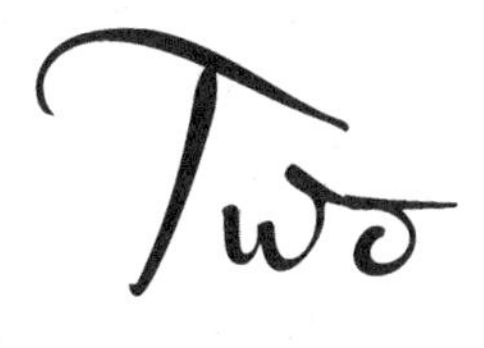

Heeding the Call

Wirral Peninsula, England, 1096

> *Narrator's note: This portion of the story was actually revealed to Amir years later by his future friend, Will. I suggested we place it here to maintain a chronological sequence of events.*

The call had gone out. In 1095, Pope Urban had invoked the Council of Clermont. Over thirty-five thousand of the faithful attended to hear his words. Among them were two hundred archbishops and bishops, four thousand ecclesiastics, and more than thirty thousand laymen. The pope spoke of the cries of Christians in the Holy Land. He told of pilgrimages that were denied, caravans attacked, the destruction of holy sites, and the murder of the faithful at the hands of the Saracen hordes. Urban called for a massive crusade of men of the cross to travel to the Holy Land and take back what was rightly the church and God's properties. Jerusalem would not be destroyed by the Saracens but would return to the Holy City where Christ had died and been resurrected. It would suffer no more defilement by these followers of Mohammed.

The council and all in attendance were so moved by Urban's

speech and the fervor it created they broke into cheers and shouts of "Deus vult! Deus vult!" (God desires it! God desires it!) The council passed many resolutions and offered absolution of sins to those who would fight and safe passage of crusaders upon pain of excommunication to any who would not assist theses defenders of the cross. Damnation to hell was the reward for any who would hinder them in any fashion.

In addition to these heavenly factors was the very real potential for plunder of the Saracen vaults. Stories had been told of massive caches of gold objects, fine gems, and rare spices. These were promised to all the faithful who took up the quest. Throughout Europe, arms were gathered along with coats of chainmail. All were blessed by the priests and sprinkled with holy water. Broadswords, axes, spears, and the deadly crossbows were carefully packed along with as much ration as the huge draft horses could carry. Hundreds of knights accompanied by thousands of men-at-arms set out for the two-hundred-day journey. Out front were the priests and bishops dedicated to the spiritual pureness of the cause and the immortal souls of the travelers. Following the knights and men-at-arms were the tradesmen; blacksmiths, carpenters, bakers, weapons bearers, healers, and barbers (surgeons of the time) walked the path set down by the crusaders. Lastly, some women and children followed their fathers, husbands, and brothers in wood-wheeled wagons pulled by farm oxen. Others followed out of sense of duty or loyalty to the Crusade. Some followed fearing thievery, mischief, and even death back home. It was in the context of service to God and Crown that Richard of Wirral and his only son, Will, joined the two-hundred-day march to Jerusalem.

Will was the only son of Richard of Wirral and Elizabeth of Wales. His mother had died bringing Will into the world. The family lineage of Will, Richard, Richard's brothers and sisters (seven in all), and the rest of his extended family were mostly Anglo-Saxon, some Welsh, some Irish, and a good portion of Norse Viking. The Norsemen had raided the shores around the Wirral Peninsula for several hundred years. Some of these Norsemen stayed on and established small colonies close to the coast and eventually were absorbed by marriage into the larger communities. Young Will had taken on his father's trade as a blacksmith and had established a reputation as an excellent ironsmith and maker of quality weapons. Will loved to watch his father work as the flames roared with each bellows compression. He marveled at his father's strength as he lifted heavy boxes of metal for horseshoes or spear tips. At twelve years of age, Will began learning his father's trade in earnest. He built and tended the fires all day, cleaned and sharpened the newly formed farm implements, and watched closely as his father shaped the swords, axes, and chain mail armor of the knights. His apprenticeship would not suffer with this crusade to the Holy Lands. He and his father were almost daily engaged in some sort of smithwork for the knights and men-at-arms. He learned to speak French while playing with the sons of French knights and Latin while attending the daily Mass and prayers. One priest, seeing the natural intelligence and inquisitiveness of young Will, taught him to write in Latin and to translate into English. Will felt he would surely become a scholar by the time he returned to Wirral. His father, Richard, approved. He was happy that his son wanted to follow his blacksmith trade, but he also knew that the free education his son was getting was unheard off back home. With the skills of the learned, Will could become a merchant or town official—or perhaps become a priest or even a bishop!

Richard, Will, and most of the other tradesmen stayed miles behind the battle lines. None of these men were warriors, yet all of them were valuable in the building and repair of war implements. The carpenters were especially busy repairing the huge siege towers. As one city would fall, the carpenters would rush in to repair or rebuild these massive structures for the next city to come under siege. The healers, barbers, and bleeders were closer to the battle lines, caring for the wounded and, in some cases, burying the dead.

It was in Damascus that many of the tradesmen set up camps

to service the crusaders laying siege to Jerusalem. It was far enough away from the engagements yet close enough to the participants to be effective. The local population was friendly enough and the local caliph wise enough to avoid the direct confrontation with the crusaders.

It was at this time that Father Joseph fled Jerusalem and the Church of the Holy Sepulcher. The priests and bishop all agreed that someone should try to flee Jerusalem, taking with them as many holy relics as could be safely transported. Father Joseph was born in Damascus, and his family was still there. The local caliph was a Fatimid and had just assisted the caliph of Jerusalem in evicting the Seljuk Turks. He neither supported nor harassed the small Christian community there, and in return, the Christians paid their taxes and did not oppose him in any instance. So Father Joseph packed a small caravan with the holy relics, manuscripts, and as many provisions for the trip as was possible for a camel to carry and set out for Damascus. The trip took over a week to complete, and he was spared the highwaymen and robbers along the route.

Father Joseph and his caravan arrived outside Damascus early one morning, much to the surprise of his family and friends who were unaware of his trip. The greetings were warm and joyous but turned serious as Father Joseph told his extended family about the trip from Jerusalem and the coming conflagration that all feared.

On the edge of the city was a small Christian abbey managed by a group of learned monks. These men were of the same Order of Scholasticism as Father Joseph, and he was welcomed as a brother. They took him deep into the catacombs of the monastery, where hidden vaults could shield the relics from those who would steal or—worse—destroy them. Among the manuscripts, objects of art, golden chalices, jeweled crosses, Bibles in Latin script, and vessels purporting to contain the bones of saints was the small, wooden box of Palestine oak that Joseph had purchased in Jerusalem. He had packed it at the last minute before he set out for Damascus. He did not know why he had packed it, but there it was, carefully wrapped in a wool cloth to protect it from the jostling of the camels as they trudged northward. As Father Joseph diligently unwrapped the wool cloth, exposing the box, he thought he had a sensation of warmth. The thought faded quickly as logic dictated that an object wrapped in wool, snuggled to the side of a camel as it trekked in the desert, would certainly be warm. He finished unpacking the relics and moved back out of the catacombs and into the light of the abbey.

It was here that Father Joseph encountered young Will of Wirral.

A Meeting with a Monk
Near Damascus, 1096

> *Narrator's note: At this point, I asked Amir to describe his thoughts regarding the earlier chain of events.*

"None of the events of those last few weeks served to cool my rage," he began. "Peddled like a cheap bauble in the Jerusalem marketplace, tossed into a room corner by an unknown and unheralded priest, wrapped in rough wool smelling of sheep, and now buried in the dank vaults of an unknown abbey. If I could only break free, I would demonstrate to all the wrath of Amir Al-Braheem! I would transform myself into the purest fire, lay waste to entire cities, and decimate human populations. I would repay all of the insults, subrogation, and imprisonment I had suffered for thousands of years. I would do all these things *if* I could break free.

"But as powerful as I was, freedom was not within my grasp. Freedom must come from outside of the box. My escape would have to originate from the same mankind on whom I wished horrors and anguish. Trickery was beneath me, and I held it in contempt as I did all of mankind. How then how was freedom ever to be found?

"An effect caused by my long imprisonment, yet almost

imperceptible to me, was an increase in patience. As my patience increased, I felt my mood lighten, if ever so slightly. I would be patient. The inquisitive nature of humans would eventually work toward my release. Some unknowing person would find the box and wonder at its contents. His curiosity would compel him to open the box, thereby destroying my imprisonment. This time would come. All I needed to do was wait and be patient."

Narrator's note: Will's story continues.

It was late in the year 1097 and Jerusalem had fallen to the crusaders. The blacksmithing of war that young Will and his father had spent almost a year fully engaged had eased and Will was eager to explore this unfamiliar land. His father, however, asked him to stay within sight of his encampment. It was still a dangerous place, and many Saracens, displaced by the fall of Jerusalem, were thought to be close by in eastern Syria. Will had seen the small abbey, and it was close enough to placate his father so it became his first choice for exploration. Will recalled with pride how much he had learned on the journey to the Holy Land. He remembered with fondness the priest who had taught him Latin and other wonders of antiquity. Perhaps a monk or even the abbot would allow him to study at the feet of these scholars. The prospect was so tantalizing as to be almost irresistible.

So on a cool and cloudy morning, young Will, with his father's blessing, wrapped himself in a warm robe and began the short walk to the abbey. The abbey was essentially a large cave over which a stone façade had been installed over a period of several hundred years. Large, brass, double doors guarded the entrance, silhouetted by stone pillars. On the right side of the right door was a small bell attached to a three-feet cord of spun camel hair. As Will approached the entrance to the abbey, he was both impressed at the stone façade and slightly fearful of what may be on the other side of those imposing brass doors! His fear was short-lived, overcome by the curiosity and promise of what lay within. Will stepped forward and tentatively grasped the camel hair cord. He held his breath and pulled weakly.

As his mind raced and curiosity grew, he expected the bell to sound like the bell of a cathedral: full, resonate, and with enough power to feel its vibration. What occurred was the small, high-pitched ting one would expect of a bell in a tailor's shop. He finally exhaled then took another breath as he waited for the bell to be answered.

In a matter of seconds, young Will heard the soft padding of footsteps approaching the doors. Time for one more breath.

The doors swung slowly open, revealing a young monk in a brown cassock. His head was slightly bowed so Will could not clearly see his face. As the monk looked up, his soft, brown eyes met Will's gaze. The monk's face was tanned but not wrinkled and worn. His nose was prominent but thin and well sculpted; his cheekbone high. Will interpreted this as evidence that the monk was perhaps Greek or Byzantine. Will addressed him in English, at which the monk's thick eyebrows rose on his broad forehead. But the monk did not answer. He only looked puzzled at the foreign words spoken by this young visitor.

Will addressed the monk again, but this time in Latin. The monk's eyes widened, and his face relaxed into a smile of recognition combined with curiosity. He did not respond to Will's words with an answer. Young Will was feeling impatient. As a Christian monk at a Christian monastery, this man had to speak Latin. Will hastily broke into a greeting in French, at which the monk threw back his head and laughed heartily. It was a grand laugh, and Will was instantly at ease. He reached forward and grasped Will's shoulders firmly but with no malice. At last, the monk spoke to Will, inquiring in perfect English as to how a young English boy he had seen many times at the encampment could speak and speak with confidence in French and Latin. Young Will was slightly embarrassed, and his neck and forehead glowed with a fresh blush. The monk introduced himself as Father Joseph and asked young Will to come inside.

Will accompanied Father Joseph into the abbey, which seemed to balloon out in volume as they walked. Father Joseph introduced Will to a group of monks just returning from morning prayers. It was a diverse group with some monks (three or four) seeming very old, gray haired, and shuffling with the gait of decades wearing down on them. Another group was about Will's father's age—upright in stance with the unblemished hands of a scholar. Lastly were several boys in their early teens with their arms full of books and manuscripts. They wore cassocks but not the large cross worn around the neck by all of the priests. As the introductions went around, Will learned that these younger tenants were students preparing for the priesthood. Will saw that many of the manuscripts were written in Greek and, he supposed, ready for translation into Latin.

He and Father Joseph walked again and entered a large room with an altar at its head. The room was lined with rough-hewn benches of wood and faced the altar. Except for Will and Father Joseph, the room—or sanctuary as Will came to know it—was empty. Father Joseph asked Will to sit and tell him how it was that a young blacksmith helper was so learned in the classical languages.

Father Joseph's manner was calm and welcoming, and Will felt no fear in telling his story of the long march from Wirral in England. Will told him about playing with the sons and squires of French knights and that if he wished to communicate with them, he had to learn French. He told him about the young priest who took it upon himself to educate Will in Latin and methods of translation. Will reckoned that he must have an aptitude for learning languages because it seemed easy. Will told of adventures, new foods, new songs, and new methodologies for treating the ill or—worse—the wounded. The traditional bleeding of a wounded warrior who was suffering from a lack of blood due to a sword strike never seemed to make much sense to him.

Father Joseph laughed again and agreed with Will that some cures were worse than the affliction. He told Will of his own love of antiquities and that these manuscripts contained the lost knowledge and science of the classic Greek and Roman philosophers. Aristotle, Archimedes, Pliny, and more giants of their age had preserved their wisdom in these manuscripts, and he and his brothers were dedicated to the preservation and translation of these people to glorify God and share with all mankind.

Will was enthralled with his new friend and asked Father Joseph to tell him his tale and how it was that he arrived at this abbey. Joseph related that he had been born very close to here to Christian parents. He had been given the Syrian Christian name of Yesopf after St. Joseph of Bethlehem. He told Will of his love of languages and his desire to study and translate the ancient manuscripts. He spoke of his education among the priests of the Church of the Holy Sepulcher in Jerusalem and how he had spirited away many artifacts, manuscripts, and holy relics to protect them from the siege of Jerusalem.

Will listened intensely, studying every word spoken by Father Joseph. He thought about asking Father Joseph's permission to visit often and study with him, but before he could ask, Father Joseph asked if he would like to learn more about the work of the abbey and the priests inside. Will shook with excitement! This would be wonderful beyond all dreams. But Father Joseph interrupted Will's delight with an admonishment that Will must ask permission from his father. Will started to speak, but Father Joseph continued. He told Will that his first duty was to help his father and only when Will's duties allowed should he come to the abbey.

Father Joseph explained that the Word tells us to respect our mothers and fathers and that he will not contravene this commandment. Will promised to speak to his father immediately and to get permission.

Will rose from his bench and started to leave when he abruptly turned and asked Father Joseph for a blessing. Father Joseph smiled and arched his thick eyebrows upward on his forehead. He made the sign of the cross, pronounced the blessing, and with war all around, sent Will out with the Latin "Pax vobiscum!"

Will covered the distance between the abbey and his encampment in what seemed like an instant. In all, he had spent most of the morning and into early afternoon with Father Joseph. He was hungry but quickly sought out his father. Young Will talked almost nonstop as he described his visit to the abbey and meeting the monks and students. He told his father about meeting the most incredible priest named Father Joseph and how this priest had promised to let Will study the ancient manuscripts and languages. He could actually work with the scholars to translate the ancient wisdom, logic, science, and healing arts!

When Richard asked about his blacksmithing duties, young Will described how Father Joseph had insisted that he have permission and that his work in the encampment would not suffer. Richard smiled and rubbed his stomach. It was only then that young Will realized how hungry he was. He happily joined his father in preparing the midday meal.

Late that afternoon, Richard crossed the distance to the abbey and rang the small bell. When the door opened, Richard was greeted by a priest who fit the description of Father Joseph. He introduced himself as Will's father then grasped Father Joseph's arms in the strong grip of a blacksmith, looked directly into the brown eyes of Father Joseph with his own fierce, blue Nordic eyes, and said only two words.

"Thank you!"

A Choice to Be Made
Near Damascus, 1099

Young Will spent the next four years balancing the blacksmith trade and his studies at the abbey with Father Joseph. Will had grown strong and tall with shoulder-length blond hair. His arms and chest were looking more like a blacksmith's than a scholar's. He was approaching his sixteenth year and looked like a man, not a boy!

His mind had expanded also. He had poured over the ancient manuscripts, absorbing every word and thought that the authors had to offer. Will became skilled in mathematics, assisting his father in the finest of measurements requiring minute calculations in the preparation of the metallic siege tower parts. He no longer had to "feel" the balance in a newly created broadsword; his measurements and geometric drawings calculated center of balance and weights needed to become an effective crusader's weapon.

Will also spent weeks investigating the ancient healing arts and the herbs that could be compounded into medicines. His knowledge of these arts spread beyond the encampment, and young Will had been called on to treat wounds and broken bones.

During the last six months, Father Joseph had let him work with the senior monks in the translation of holy texts from multiple languages of antiquity to Latin. To be allowed to work side by side with these scholars was a joy beyond description!

It was in early November that Will's father approached him to announce they were going home to England. This announcement came as a shock as Will knew that battles were still being fought and that the need for his father's skills (and his own skills) had not ended. But Richard explained that others were coming to take their places and that their kinsmen back in Wirral needed the extended family to gather. Richard's brothers had found favor with King William II, and tales told by returning men-at-arms and priests of Richard and young Will's exploits and service to the crusaders increased that favor. A plot of land had been given by the king to Richard and his brothers. This was extraordinarily rare in that most land still belonged to the nobles. But one certain nobleman had fallen out of favor with the king and ended up hanged in the White Tower in London. The lands were confiscated by King Edward and passed along to the "Wirral family and all that belong therein for their service to God and the Crown." The land would give the extended family areas for gardens and grazing for sheep. It would also allow for the construction of many houses and outbuildings for current and future generations. It was an unheard-of opportunity for a family of tradesmen to grow beyond the economic conditions of the age.

Young Will listened and understood his father's description and joyous account of what lay before them back home. But his heart was troubled. What of his studies with Father Joseph? He had learned so much, but there was so much more to learn. There were manuscripts he had not read and wisdom that had not been revealed by their authors. What would become of all of this? Richard saw the pain and despair on the face of his son. Young Will was almost a man in the eyes of his father, and Richard knew that he should not compel Will to return even though it was his father' desire. Young Will's knees felt weak and unstable. His mind was a maze of questions and probabilities. He loved his father dearly and would obey him if he made that decision that they must return.

His father saw this turmoil and uncertainty on his son's face, and it was then that he told young Will to go to the abbey and seek Father Joseph. "Tell the priest of our situation and solicit his advice and guidance." Then and only then would they make any decisions, and the decisions would be made together.

Young Will felt his wobbly legs begin to steady. He raised his head and met his father's gaze. Richard clasped his son's shoulders with that strong but comforting grip Will needed. This was the grip that had awakened him from the nightmares of childhood and comforted him during sicknesses. Will felt the strength return to his limbs and the haze of his thoughts sharpen. He smiled and turned toward the abbey.

Father Joseph listened intently as Will explained his father's announcement and his own reaction to the announcement. Father Joseph did not interrupt as Will unleased a flurry of fears, uncertainties, and rhetorical questions with no easy answers.

At some length when young Will had finally given voice to everything that was troubling him, Father Joseph offered a solution. He explained that this offering was "a" solution, not necessarily "the" solution. Will eagerly asked him to reveal the idea and bring him some peace in his troubled brain. Father Joseph smiled, arching those heavy eyebrows high on his forehead, and began to speak.

It was twilight before young Will returned to the encampment and his father.

Richard had thrown a robe around his clothing to protect against the November chill. He had also given the bellows a few compressions to brighten the fire. He was happy to see Will's approach and hoped Father Joseph had offered some advice and guidance to his son. As young Will drew nearer to the fire, his father could see a look of peace but also of purpose on Will's face. The visage of confusion, fear, and conflict was gone, and Will looked satisfied and hopeful. He told his father of Father Joseph's words that he saw a different destiny for Will. Father Joseph continued that he had always felt his destiny was to learn from, translate, and protect the ancient manuscripts and relics. He was happy and fulfilled in this role and that he wished for no other avocation.

But Will he saw in a different light. Will's education at the abbey in addition to his experiences with multiple cultures made him supremely prepared to return to his home and teach these great secrets of antiquity to his fellow men. To study and protect was an excellent destiny. To teach, dispense, and disperse the philosophy and science he had acquired was a superior destiny. Father Joseph told Will that he had feelings that came to him as dreams in the night that Will would play a part in some significant events of the future. It was never clear what those events might be, but Father Joseph knew in his heart and soul that Will's presence, knowledge, and wisdom would be called upon.

> *Narrator's note: At this point, I stopped transcribing and asked Amir if he was responsible for the content of Father Joseph's dreams. He smiled that canine, tooth-filled grin and asked that we continue.*

"Young Will reached into his bag and retrieved a small box which he handed to his father. The box was one inch square with a sealed lid. Richard recognized it as being made from Palestine oak. Father Joseph had made the box a parting gift for Will. He told Will of buying the "relic" from a seller in the ancient walled city of Jerusalem, close to the site of Solomon's temple. He told Will of the seller's claim that the box possessed and contained an ancient magic, protected by curses and dire predictions. Father Joseph admitted to Will that he had not witnessed any supernatural occurrences surrounding the box, but he hoped it would remind Will of his time at the abbey.

"Father Joseph also gave Will a small bag of medicinal herbs that had been collected from the local fields and also traded from the caravans of the east. Some of these herbs had been gathered by shamans of the great mountains and terraced valleys of strange cultures found along the Silk Road to China. Will had been tutored in the use of these medicines and knew of their rarity and value. Will told Father Joseph how his time at the abbey would always be remembered with honor and wonder. He considered these as the best times of his young life and he would study, protect, and treasure these gifts.

"Will and Father Joseph clasped each other's shoulders, smiled at each other, and turned away. They would never see each other again.

"Richard listened to his son and examined the small box and bag of herbs. He spoke softly to Will that these were wonderful gifts and that Father Joseph's guidance gave evidence to his wisdom. The father and son embraced each other, content in the pathways ahead: Richard to his family's new lands and enterprises and young Will to a destiny that was still being defined. Richard returned the box to Will, noticing a slight warmth that seemed to emanate. It was quickly forgotten. They would pack over the next few days and set out toward England with a compliment of returning crusaders, men-at-arms, families, and priests.

"The journey of over two hundred days would yield several surprises regarding the small box of Palestine oak and me, who was inside."

The Road Home
Antioch, 1100

> *Narrator's note: Will's story continues with Amir's interjections.*

"It was on the road to Antioch that Will first perceived something odd about the small, wooden box. His habit was to keep the box in a leather pouch that hung from his waist. Will would not trust the swaying packs on the camels to fully protect his relic. I was fully aware of Father Joseph's gift to Will. It was all the better to be freed of the scholar/priest who stored the box in the damp catacombs of the abbey. At least in Will's pouch, I could sense the surroundings. As jinn, I drew my sustenance (oxygen, carbon, hydrogen, nitrogen, and other elements and natural compounds) from the earth and atmosphere. And here in a soft, leather bag at the boy's waist (I began to refer to Will as 'the boy'), I began to become more aware of the outside world. I could feel the desert warmth and sense the thoughts of those in the caravan.

"All jinn possessed telepathic powers, and I delighted in entering the dreams of those who slept nearby and thought it great fun to awaken a crusader with a particularly nasty and vivid nightmare!

Many nights, these terrors would awaken the dreamer who would shout and cry out! Many others in the band of travelers would waken and the dreams would be told to the amazement of all who heard. The priests prayed that whatever spirit was bringing these dreams would depart. I could not depart.

"I did not visit Will in the night. The boy treated the box as a revered relic to be protected and cared for. This particular human was cultured and intelligent. But most of all, he was respectful of the relic and therefore respectful of its contents. I felt I could tolerate the boy and would send no dreams of horror and death to trouble his sleep.

"As the travelers camped outside the city of Antioch, Will wished to explore the area and perhaps enter the city. His father admonished him to be aware of those that preyed on travelers, even those under protection of the pope. Will promised that he would be cautious and turned toward the city.

In the previous years, Richard saw that Will was becoming powerful even as he was physically powerful. The years of lifting and carrying heavy metals for the forge made Will strong. Richard's friends and even some of the knights would joke with him that if an ox became lame, they could hitch its load to Will. Richard took the jests as they were intended: compliments. Will would be fine in his explorations if he kept his wits and remembered his physical strength.

Antioch was a natural crossroads between east and west. There were always caravans traveling through with camels and oxcarts piled high with valuables of the time. Spices, rare woods, jewels, carpets, and exotic foods were a sampling of the riches carried by the merchants. But where there are riches, there are thieves, and Antioch was no different. The merchants traveled with well-armed guards and paid the local officials a special fee for safe right-of-way. Will had no such entourage.

"Will explored the encampments circling the city and, with his mastery of languages, conversed with many travelers. He learned of their homes and their destinations. He was offered small tastings of the exotic foods and spices and regaled with harrowing tales of the caravan. Will thanked his hosts, said the prayers for their safe travels, and turned toward the city gates.

"He was only about one hundred yards from entering the city when a group of four men rose from their campfire and encircled Will. Will observed that the men were young, probably in their late teens. All carried daggers on their belts, but none had swords. They were thin faced, dark skinned, and probably Saracen. Will spoke first in Greek, greeting them and inquiring about their intentions. The four stared at Will, not understanding his words. Arabic was Will's least practiced language, but he repeated the words in Arabic to the full understanding of the four.

"One of the four (the largest and possibly the leader) asked Will if he was a crusader returning from Jerusalem. He said that crusaders were returning with spoils and lootings from Islamic mosques and that he must pay a ransom for taking these items. As the four tightened their circle around Will, the leader pointed to Will's leather pouch at his waist and questioned if it held gold and silver coins. In his best Arabic, Will told the four that he was not a crusader but a blacksmith apprentice and he had no coins of any type. He said the contents in the pouch were gifts from a priest of little or no monetary value.

"A sneer formed on the face of the leader, and he spoke through his teeth, telling Will to hand over the pouch or die. Will tensed his muscles and prepared to fight. He sensed that even if he gave them the pouch, the four would attack him. Will's eyes narrowed and shone their fierce, Nordic blue. He crouched slightly and in his best Arabic bid all four go straight to hell.

"I was slightly amused at the confrontation. Were I free, a simple gesture would have sent the four into instant agonies from the hottest flames. I was also slightly annoyed that the boy had described the contents of his pouch as having little to no worth. No worth indeed! However lightly that I assessed the confrontation, I did not belittle the possibility of the box being captured by the hooligans. I did not care to be handled by thieves. The box was too small to contain many coins so they would probably sell it to some other felons or worse. I was not thrilled with the prospect. But what if they broke the sealed lid and freed me? Of course all four would perish at my hands instantly!

"My thoughts swirled around my head like the clouds of a whirling dervish. Solomon, with the ring provided by the Most High and delivered by the archangel Gabriel, had imprisoned me. What if destruction of the box would cause the destruction of me? Perhaps there was some secret sequence of events in opening the box that would free me? Could it be that my destiny was to be destroyed by thieves? Solomon would enjoy that ending of a powerful jinn.

"Two of the four attacked Will at once—one from the right and one from the left. They had drawn their daggers and screams of battle issued from their throats. Will pivoted to the left and the forearm of a blacksmith met the throat of an attacker. The force of the attack combined with the power of Will's forearm sent the first attacker flat in the air, landing harshly on his back with his larynx crushed and gasping for life-sustaining air. The attacker on the right hesitated long enough for Will to step into his attackers' path and, with a powerful upward motion of his clenched fists (as in lifting a box of horseshoes), find the attacker's chin, driving his lower jaw upward and into his skull. In the process, the attacker bit through his tongue and crushed most of his diseased teeth. The force of Will's strike lifted the attacker upward and backward as he landed on his back with a sickening thud!

"As all this was transpiring, the attacker in the rear engaged at his fullest speed, crouching and hitting Will in the back of his knees. Will was thrust forward, down to his knees with the force of the attacker weighing Will down to the dirt. It was then that the front attacker dropped down on Will's shoulders and put the dagger to his throat. He was pinned around the legs and now the shoulders. He could not move or defend himself any longer. One quick thought of his father and Father Joseph, and Will was ready to die.

"As the leader pressed the dagger into Will's jugular vein, I entered his mind and the leader's brain became inflamed with the scene of a dark and dank dungeon. It was filled with every viper, asp, and cobra in nature, and all were striking him in the face, neck, torso, genitals, and legs. As he opened his mouth to scream, large constrictors issued forth, biting his eyes and encircling him with their deadly coils. Scorpions emerged from his ears and stung his lips and tongue. The leader dropped his dagger and rose to his feet. He was holding his face with both hands and screaming an unearthly howl of horror. He ran into the desert, still screaming as his mind approached insanity. The attacker who had tackled Will rolled to his right, sprang to his feet, and was gone in seconds.

"Some people from the caravans had heard the screams and came to investigate. They found Will standing erect, a man on the ground in obvious agony, sucking small gulps of air, and another crawling away sobbing incoherently. Will told his new friends of the caravan what had happened but could not explain why the leader of the four ceased his slicing of Will's throat and ran, screaming into the desert. All were amazed at the story and insisted on accompanying Will back to his father's encampment. Will reached for the leather pouch and found it secured to his belt and firmly around his waist. He did notice that it was hot to the touch.

"It was me! I had intervened," he said as he laughed. "It was me that had put the vision of the asps and cobras into the subconscious of the hooligan. I was quite capable of occupying the feeble brains of mankind and inserting all manner of terror. No one had seen what the leader had seen. But to this unfortunate thief, it was all real. The visions lasted only several seconds but were so horrifying that the thief could only stumble away, whimpering softly, still hearing the sounds of his own screams.

"Will returned to his encampment and told the tale to his father and friends. They were glad at his safe return, amazed at the turn of events, and swore to arrange a party of men-at-arms to accompany Will on any more explorations. Richard hugged his son tightly and struggled with thoughts that Will could have been lost. Richard slept fitfully that night, playing the events of the day over and over in his mind. He vowed to himself that grown man or no, he would allow no harm to come to his son.

"I allowed Will slept soundly that night. He suffered no dreams or replaying of events. When he rose with the morning sun, he did have thoughts about the thief, pinning him, facedown, pulling his head upward by the hair, and preparing to roughly draw the dagger across his throat. Why did he stop? Why did he rise off my shoulders, grasp his head with both hands, and scream as if in agony? Will had no answers or theories. Father Joseph had spoken of destinies. Will concluded that it was not his destiny to die at Antioch. Then what was his destiny, and why had the box (cool now) been so hot?

"No matter. Will vowed not to travel unarmed again. With his father's permission, Will began to forge a very special sword. He remembered the ancient texts on metallurgy and combined them with the available ores of the day to produce an alloy that was light, extraordinarily strong, and had the property of maintaining an edge not found in weapons of the day. It was about three feet long with a pointed tip for thrusting, and it had a double edge for slashing in the forehand or backhand. Its balance was superb! The sword resembled a xiphos that had accompanied the Spartans into battle but was much lighter. Will fashioned a leather cover for the sword and a leather belt from which it could be suspended. If attacked again, he would give a better account of himself."

Six

The Road to Constantinople
Asia Minor, late 1100

> *Narrator's note: Amir and I had been at this record and transcribe marathon for several days and my strength and stamina (along with my appetite) had steadily improved. I remembered his words "Write and live!"*

"The leader of the caravan insisted (in his best English) that Will, his father, and the returning knights, men-at-arms, and all the rest of them travel with him to Constantinople. The leader's name was Fahad, and he came from the lands east of Persia. His caravan was made up of Muslims from Baghdad, Coptic Christians from Egypt, Armenian Christians from Asia Minor, and various other cultures and creeds. The road to Constantinople was in Seljuk Turk territory, but the Turks typically allowed the caravans to pass (trading for spices and rare, bejeweled arms). Fahad argued that his caravan of fifty combined with Will's party of thirty well-armed and experienced warriors, plus the tradesmen and their families, would put off any highwaymen and scoundrels on the prowl to seize goods from honest traders. Richard waited to make sure he understood the broken English, looking to Will for his interpretation, and then agreed to wild sounds and high trills of joy and jubilation from the members of the caravan. They would indeed be a formidable group to attack. Fahad exclaimed that it was settled and that all of them would depart for Constantinople at the sunrise.

"It would take four weeks to traverse the distance from Antioch to Constantinople. Much to everyone's delight, the trip was without incident and the group traveled steadily toward the Bosporus. For Will, one of the joys of the trip was at days end when all gathered around a large campfire and cooked the evening meal. What a wonderful mélange of foods from the entire known world. Each cultural group was excited to offer up a specific delicacy and get reaction from the travelers. There were grains ready to fry in exotic oils, milk and cheeses from the dromedaries in the caravan, and meats dried and seasoned from the eastern regions of the world. Will's group would add local game birds and deer, and all would marvel at the bounty!

"At the end of the meal, someone would break into a story.

"The Christians would scare up tales of fallen angels, vampires, and the incubus and succubus that sought out men's souls through sexual intercourse during sleep. For the sexually denied crusaders and travelers, these were especially interesting. The Muslims would regale the group with stories of King Solomon's mines and tales from what would become *1001 Arabian Nights* and the *Rubaiyat* of Omar Khayyam. Will was especially intrigued by stories of the jinn and their interactions with mankind. But Fahad warned Will not to pursue knowledge of the jinn and pointed to verses in the Koran outlining prayers to protect oneself from actions of the jinn. Even so, I could tell Will was intrigued.

"Several days out from Antioch, one of the Arab traders' children fell ill. Will knew the trader only as Mohammed (as many men took the name of the Prophet) and his child as Benazir. She was about nine years old and usually running roughshod over her male playmates. One day, Will missed her playing with the other children. He dismissed her absence on perhaps her being called for some duty in service to her family. This was not unusual since most of the children traveling with the caravan members had to work at some chore, be it sewing and repairing clothes or tents or preparing food that would be served at the evening meal. Sometimes the older ones were tasked to care for their brothers or sisters or feed and water the caravan's animals. It was not until Fahad approached Will and Richard on an evening after a full day's travel, accompanied by Mohammed, that Will thought there may be something wrong with the child.

"Fahad called out a greeting and asked Will to speak with Mohammed. Mohammed came near Will with his head bowed and in obvious distress. Will spoke the traditional greeting of 'Peace be unto you,' at which Mohammed returned the greeting and began to speak. Benazir had fallen ill two days before. Mohammed thought it was a passing illness of childhood, but then she began burning with fever and was unable to eat. She complained loudly about a sore throat and how it hurt to swallow so much that she refused to drink. Members of his tribe had seen this in children before and knew that some children beat back the fever and that many did not and died from it.

"He could not understand what evil spirit or humor imbalance could have caused this. Fahad had spoken of Will's knowledge of the healing arts dating back to antiquity and the most modern of methods from the monks at the abbey outside Antioch. Mohammed raised his head and his wide brown eyes met Will's gaze. What price would Will charge to keep his Benazir from death?

"Will assessed the plea from Mohammed and his description of Benazir's symptoms. He reached out to Mohammed with both arms, clasping the Arab as one would an old friend, and told Mohammed that there is no price as dear as the loss of a loved one. Will said that he would use the knowledge and medicines given to him by Father Joseph to return Benazir to full health and her father's company. When Will had finished speaking, Mohammed dropped to his knees and wept uncontrollably. Will reached down to help Mohammed to his feet and asked them to lead him to Benazir.

"It was mid-December and snows had fallen on the hills and peaks along the road to Constantinople. Will asked two men-at-arms to go to the hills, about an hour's walk away, to gather snow in empty waterskins. They were to pack the snow as full as possible and then wrap the bags with blankets for insulation. The men set out to gather the snow. Will asked that a special tent be erected for the treatment of Benazir. He searched back to the lessons Father Joseph taught about this particular fever and silently prayed that as Hippocrates had commanded, he did not make things worse.

"The tent went up and Benazir was brought inside and placed on a bed of camel robes. The child was pale, hot to the touch, and her skin was dry. She expelled a dry cough, moved in and out of consciousness, and writhed in her discomfort.

"Will drew the camel robes tightly around her and asked that a small fire be prepared in the center of the tent. As the flames of the fire grew, Will doused the flames with water containing oil of eucalyptus and menthol. Steam arose and filled the tent with the rich scent of medicinal vapors. He stoked the fire again and boiled a small portion of tree bark from a willow in a vessel of water. By this time, the men had returned with the skins packed with snow. Will emptied a portion of the snow into a small cup and put it to Benazir's lips. The child quickly took the chilling snow water and swallowed weakly. He knew that he must get water into the feverish child, and by sipping on the melted snow, her pain at swallowing was decreased.

"Will then took the potion of boiled tree bark and added it to the melted snow for Benazir to drink. He reached into his medicinal bag and brought forth a small pack of ground and distilled blue mold. The smell was strong and the child turned away from it. Will held her nose and poured the brew along with the melting snow into her mouth. Benazir coughed and spat but had to swallow a portion of the compounds. Will continued this process for the next four hours until he saw what he had been looking for: a small but increasing bead of sweat began to form on Benazir's forehead. Will himself was drenched in his own sweat and in bad need of water to replenish his loss. Benazir, however, broke into a full and copious sweat as her fever broke and her body temperature began to return to normal. He remained with her and kept her supplied with large amounts of melting snow to drink along with the willow bark brew.

"The next day, an exhausted Will emerged from the tent with a very much improved Benazir in his arms. Upon seeing this, Mohammed rushed to Will and retrieved his daughter, crying and wailing in utmost joy. The entire caravan and camp woke to the news of Benazir's recovery at the hands of Will. There was much celebration and amazement that Benazir, who appeared on death's door, had been restored to health. Will was lauded as a great healer and mystic but he took no such honors. All of his skills were taught to him by Father Joseph, who had translated the ancient texts to extract this knowledge of healing. However, none would hear his entreaties. To all, he was Will the Healer! To his father, he was a son of many talents. It was difficult for Richard to conceal his pride.

"I sensed all of this and remained silent. No warmth emanated from the box or nightmares haunt the group. I felt a keen sense of achievement for Will, and if it could be described in a way, I had a small semblance of pride in this human who acted with such skill and dignity. The boy was obviously special among his kind and I would not take away from this triumph. I did enter the dreams of Benazir and favor her with dreams of meadows and sheep, trees and cool breezes as the last of her affliction departed. I also left a permanent picture of Will in her dream as the man who saved her. As for Will, I gifted him with a deep and dreamless sleep.

"The next few days passed without issue or ailment, and miles to Constantinople became few and fewer. One evening after a good day's journey, Will saw Fahad coming toward his campfire, accompanied by Mohammed and little Benazir. Fahad raised his right hand with shouts of 'Peace be with you!' as Benazir ran past the men and into the surprised arms of Will! She hugged him tightly about the neck as her father admonished her to remember her manners. She finally released Will from the hug and he rose to his feet and returned Fahad's greeting with 'And unto you!' Will asked the party to come sit and warm themselves by his fire, and Fahad, Mohammed, and Benazir circled the fire and sat down with Benazir closest to Will. He looked at her and could tell that her ailment was completely gone. She looked strong and happy as her large brown eyes looked into Will's blue eyes. Fahad was first to speak. He told how his friend Mohammed was forever in Will's debt and that he had restored a father's most precious possession. Will faced Mohammed and bowed his head slightly, acknowledging the compliment. Fahad continued that this was not the reason for their visit tonight. Again Will faced Mohammed and asked in his best Arabic what was troubling Mohammed. Mohammed was highly troubled! His head was held low, and he seemed to struggle to meet Will's gaze. When he spoke, Mohammed's voice was barely audible and his speech was choppy as he drew in small gulps of air. Will encouraged Mohammed to speak freely. Mohammed glanced briefly over at Fahad and began.

"Benazir had been having dreams. Will's expression narrowed with concern, but Mohammed, still troubled, clarified that the dreams were described by Benazir as happy, pleasant, and full of rich smells, textures, and colorful vistas. Mohammed raised his head to meet Will's eyes and asked who dreams like this. No dreams by his family members had ever been described with this detail and involving so many senses.

"Another detail described by Mohammed was that Benazir did not forget the dreams. Most dreams he had ever heard about were ephemeral and faded quickly after awakening. It was as if Benazir were reading from an illustrated text! Mohammed also found it unusual that she would remember Will and his efforts to save her. After all, she was racked by fever and in and out of a conscious state. But the most troubling description by Benazir was the very tall man made of fire. She said he was handsome and seemed very powerful but that she was not afraid. The man of fire had taken her hand and led her to a wonderful field filled with grass and flowers. Benazir thought that the man of fire's hands might burn her but that when he touched her, his hand of fire turned blue and was cool as streams of water in the mountains.

"She asked the man of fire if she could play with the lambs grazing in the field and that he had told her do so as long as she liked. After a while, the man of fire told her it was time to return to her father. She said she was sad to leave but happy to rejoin her father. She then described how the man of fire gently commanded her to remember all that had happened and especially remember the young man with fierce blue eyes and golden hair named Will. She should remember that it was Will who had saved her.

"Will and Richard looked at Fahad and Mohammed in astonishment and said nothing. It was Fahad who spoke and told them what was troubling Mohammed. They were both in fear that Benazir had been visited by the jinn. At the mention of this legendary being, Mohammed began to shake violently! He asked why one so powerful would wish harm on his child. He said the jinn were jealous of mankind and always looking for ways to heap misery and doom upon us in their rage at being imprisoned by Allah at the hand of Solomon.

"It was Will who soothed the moment. He told them of legends of jinn who did not fall with Lucifer and wished no harm to mankind. He told them of the parallel existence of the jinn and that they were unlikely to interact with mankind. Lastly, he said he neither saw nor felt any evil presence as he treated Benazir or in the description of her dreams. Will asked that Mohammed monitor his daughter for the next few days and see if the dreams dissipate. It could be as easily explained that her dreams were an unforeseen effect of the medicines. Regardless, if Benazir's dreams faded, Will foresaw no long-term effects.

"Will's words and explanations seemed to mollify Mohammed and Fahad somewhat, and they rose to return to the caravan's encampment. Will asked Mohammed if he could speak to Benazir for a few moments alone. Mohammed was a bit uneasy at this request but agreed and began his walk back. Will turned to Benazir, who seemed to be the only one not terrified or astonished, to ask her one question about her dreams. Benazir smiled broadly and told Will to ask his question. Will's query to Benazir was when she dreamed of him helping her with cool water and medicines, where had the man of fire come from? Benazir bent down and pointed to the pouch on Will's waist. Will quickly opened the pouch and brought forth the small box of Palestine oak. Benazir looked at the box and then up at him as she answered his question.

"From there!"

> *Narrator's note: I could see a distinct change in Amir's mood as he told this story. He seemed to develop an affection for Will and Benazir. An affection less like one between people and more like between a person and a pet.*

Seven

Two Bitter Losses
Constantinople, January 1101

"The caravan arrived in Constantinople about the time of celebration of Christ's birth. Twelfth Night had already begun in England. But here in the Eastern Orthodox lands, it was just beginning. The caravan and returning crusaders band had hired boats to take them across the Bosporus and into the great city of Constantinople. The city was alive with travelers, merchants, pilgrims of every nature, and mariners from the oceans of the world. Venetian mariners and traders thrived in the open commerce of the city. Long caravans arrived and departed, carting goods and riches to be traded all over the world.

"The city which had seen multiple invasions, massacres, and sieges was at peace. It was the time of the Komnenian Dynasty. A firm central government was in control and commerce was encouraged and even worshipped to a degree. The total population was approaching four hundred thousand, which made the city one of the most important places in the known world. It was said that more currency (gold, silver, metallic ores, spices, rare woods, and gemstones) changed hands here than in any other city.

"It was here in Constantinople that Fahad, Mohammed, and the rest of the caravan would turn to a destination not in the crusaders path. The caravan would move north into Serbia and the steppes of Asia to trade their goods. The crusaders and families would move west into Byzantium, taking advantage of the mild weather to cross into Europe and finally home. Fahad and all in the caravan gathered at the encampment of the crusaders to wish them well in their journeys. Richard and many of the knights offered gifts and well wishes to Fahad and his band of traders. They would be sorely missed. Fahad and the traders reciprocated with gifts of spices and carpets, rare jewels, fine robes, and best of all, foods of the east that would not be found once the crusaders arrived home.

"Will was resplendent in his robes, gifts from Mohammed, and strikingly handsome with his new sword suspended from his belt. Benazir ran to Will and he dropped to his knees to receive her embrace. She whispered that she would not forget him and had he not been so many years in advance of her, she would make him her betrothed. Will received her embrace and promised her that her future husband must be a prince in order to deserve her attention. Benazir giggled and released Will from her hug. As she walked back toward the caravan and her father, she waved a goodbye at Will, which he returned. The caravan moved away to the north, and Will never saw any of the band again.

"The group of thirty now seemed small and lonely. The exotic smells of meals and rich languages were gone. There was nothing left but to provision the group and begin the walk across Byzantium. Richard and Will were asked by the knights to bargain with the local merchants in buying provisions for the next phase of their journey. Will's knowledge of languages and Richard's bargaining skills were sure to obtain a favorable outcome. In preparation, Will loosened the belt from which the small leather pouch was attached and carefully stored it with the rest of his possessions in his tent. Will reached up to a hanger on the main tent pole and retrieved his new sword and sheath. He joined his father and they walked toward a commercial area within the city and began to seek out the provisions they would need.

"Will found a purveyor of grains that would make fine loaves of bread. He also located a trader in dried meats and fruits, ready for travel. Casks of water and of wine were bartered, and all manner of foodstuffs were attained for the journey across Byzantium. With their tasks completed and deliveries set for the morning, Richard and Will started the trip back to their encampment.

"What neither Will nor Richard saw were the five bandits in hiding. The five were of unknown origins but clever and swift in their endeavors. They would use a crossbow to kill one, then the other pilgrim silently. They would then move in quietly, taking all the valuables they could carry, and vanish into the night. After all, who would miss two pilgrims in a city filled with pilgrims?

"Richard and Will talked easily as they made their way back when suddenly Will felt a strap on his sandal break. As he bent down, he heard the unmistaken hiss of a crossbow arrow being fired followed by the short thud of the arrow striking a tree behind him. An audible curse came from the brushes in front of them followed by the ratchet of a crossbow stringer being engaged. Will's father understood these sounds as well and drew his heavy broadsword as he stepped toward the brush in front of him. Richard raised the broadsword high and to the right of his shoulder, then brought it downward at a forty-five-degree angle. The effect was to decapitate and partially eviscerate one bandit. There was no cry of pain, only the dull sound of a bodiless head hitting the ground. Richard continued the slashing movement of the broadsword by pulling it back to the left and striking another bandit in his right arm. The flesh and bone of the arm gave way and fell to the ground as a scream issued from the brush, telling Richard of a true strike.

"During this time, Will drew his Xiphos and flanked the brush ahead of them. He glimpsed the flash of a dagger in the moonlight and with a quick slash of the deadly, lightweight sword, removed the dagger filled hand of his attacker from its arm. Another scream and footsteps running away filled Will's ears. Richard pulled back the broadsword to a ready position: handle near the heart and blade pointing skyward as he searched for the next target. The next sound was a horrible click as the crossbow was fully pulled and locked. The second sound was the hiss of the boltlike arrow slicing through the air, culminating in a muffled grunt as it struck its target.

"Richard's eyes widened and his mouth opened to emit a rush of air from his lungs. He dropped and momentarily kneeled motionlessly before crashing to the ground. Will screamed an unholy oath and charged into the brush to find the crossbowman who was frantically trying to string another bolt and the last bandit who was turning to run away. Will launched into a forward roll and upon righting himself slashed the Achilles tendon of the runner. Another scream of agony and the bandit crashed to the ground, unable to stand or run.

"Then Will turned and faced the killer of his father. The bandit was small, with his face covered by a scarf to hide his identity. The bandit, still struggling with the crossbow, raised his eyes in terror. Will made a single strike to the center of the bandit's chest. The Xiphos pierced the breastbone then punctured the heart. The terrified eyes of the bandit widened like saucers then dulled as Will drew the Xiphos down into the bandit' bowels. The only sound that came from the bandit was a thick gurgling issuing from his throat. As Will drew the sword back, the bandit fell forward, facedown. Only after all were dispatched did he turn toward his father.

"Will reached his father and turned him over to assess the wounds. He could feel no pulse in his father's neck, no breath was issuing from his lungs, and his pupils were immovable and dilated. Richard was gone. The enormity of the situation was settling into Will's brain, and he dropped to his knees beside his father's lifeless body. Stifling grief enveloped Will's mind as it struggled to understand what had just happened. Salty tears filled Will's eyes and he screamed toward the sky. The grief seemed unbearable, yet another emotion began to stir inside him. It was small at first but grew quickly to a fiery rage that blocked out the grief along with all rational thought. Will rose to his feet and turned toward the fallen bowman.

"Rage animated Will's body and he shook as he found the bandit and crossbow. He drew the Xiphos and with one quick slash beheaded the dead body. As the bodiless head rolled to one side, the cloth that had been covering the bandit's face fell away. It was the face of a young girl, perhaps in her midteens, eyes open and staring at Will. A terrible thought crossed his mind that she resembled Benazir. His rage was extinguished in an instant. The horrible grief returned and now there was a sickness that enveloped him.

"Will turned away from the girl's staring eyes and spewed forth the soured contents of his stomach. He fell to the ground hard and rolled on to his back, staring at the heavens. His mind was coming to terms with these events and he realized that he had not only lost his father but also his innocence. Members of the caravan had called him 'Will the Healer.' Now he had become 'Will the Butcher.' He screamed again, but the animation of his rage was gone. His scream became a whimper as his mind tried to resolve the unresolvable. The sickness came to him again, but he only heaved dryly.

"It was morning when members of the returning crusaders and men-at-arms came to retrieve the body of Richard. Will had struggled back to his camp and told the tale to his party. They listened, the priests prayed, and all embraced Will with words of sorrow and condolence. It helped, but not much. Will had his father's body wrapped in his finest robes and laid on a rough-hewn, wooden bench. He placed several of his father's most valued blacksmith tools, which was the custom of the times, around the body and his father's broadsword across his chest.

"The priests counseled Will that Richard needed a Christian burial and that there were several appropriate sites nearby. Instead, Will told the priests of a story his father had told him about the death of a Norse king. In the story, the Norse king was laid upon a wooden raft, filled with kindling wood, and surrounded by possessions he may need in the afterlife. The raft was then pushed out into the sea or a lake. As it floated away, a family member would shoot a flaming arrow into the raft, igniting it and all that was upon it. The family would watch as the loved one was consumed and the smoke and flames lifted his soul to God. Will told them this was his father's wish and that it would be done. The priests warned that this was a pagan practice and that they could not bless it. Will turned and smiled at the priests. He reminded them that the crusaders and all that traveled with them had been absolved of all sins, past and future by no less than the Holy See in Rome. Will repeated that his father's wish would be fulfilled. There was no further discussion.

"The arrangements were made, the raft prepared, and all were in attendance (even the priests) as Will said his final farewell to his father and the raft was launched into a quiet bay opening to the blue Mediterranean Sea. Since Will was no bowman, he asked one of the English men-at-arms to shoot the flaming arrow in his place. The bowman lit the arrow and drew back his English longbow and let it fly. The flaming arrow streaked across the sky in a large arc then landed squarely on the raft, igniting it. All watched as the flames grew to envelope the raft and consume it. In a matter of minutes, the raft started breaking apart and sinking. Above it rose a column of gray smoke heavenward.

"On the way back to the encampment, the bowman who had shot the flaming arrow asked Will why he did not wear the fine Xiphos that he had crafted. Will answered that it was on his father's burial raft and he hoped it had become consumed by the fires. The bowman asked why Will would do such a thing, to which Will replied that he was a blacksmith and occasional healer and that as such, he had no need of such weapons. The bowman shook his head in bewilderment and departed. When Will returned to his tent, he reached for and retrieved the belt and leather pouch and tied it around his waist. As soon as the pouch and box inside touched Will's body, I leapt into Will's thoughts. I saw it all: the terror, butchery, death, grief, and my old companion's rage!

"I was instantly saddened by what 'the boy' just experienced. Humans were weak and fragile, unlike me. I had a fleeting thought about communicating with the boy, but maybe later when things had calmed. A gentle warmth began to radiate from the box."

Eight

A Being of Fire

Western Byzantine Empire, January 1101

> *Narrator's note: This portion of the story is Amir's recollection of Will's impression of their first meeting.*

"The days went by as did the miles traveled. Will waited for the misery and sadness to lessen. It did not! The single blessing that seemed to come from the violence and loss of the attack on Will and his father was that every night since; he had slept soundly and not dwelled on the recent history of the recent events. He thought it was as if someone or something sponged away the memories of his father's death and the rage that caused him to behead a dead child. His dreams were of home and sometimes Damascus. The people in his dreams were mild, friendly, and familiar but abstract in their purpose. The dream people were always smiling at him and wishing him good day. But when the daylight arrived and he arose, the sadness, bitterness and loses returned and enveloped him. The priests and some of Will's companions observed Will's melancholy and wondered if he could ever fully recover. Many tried to engage him in conversation about his favorite topics: ancient manuscripts, classical sciences, and languages. Will would smile at them, listen for a moment, then drift slowly away back into his gray, dark exile.

"The travelers had only a few more days walk to the shores of the Adriatic Sea and a crossing onto the boot heel of Italy. An advance party had been sent to procure boats for the passage and landing at Brindisi. Once in Italy, they would resupply their provisions and set their path toward Rome. There was an excitement building among the returning crusaders and other travelers at the chance that while in Rome, they were to be invited to an audience with the Holy Father. They had heard rumors that all would be blessed and that certain treasures would be awarded to those who had answered Pope Urban's call at Claremont. Papal lands were to be divided among the faithful, bad marriages could be annulled, and cardinals appointed. For the less lofty in the band of travelers were sacks of gold and silver, looted from the mosques and cities of the Saracen. Many of the treasures were brought to Rome and pledged to the Holy Father and the church by crusaders returning earlier. They too had brought tribute to the pope from the Holy Lands. But wise crusaders made sure that they and their entourage kept sufficient compensation for their labors—just in case the rumors were not true. Will and his father had been paid well for the blacksmithing done in support of the crusaders and had amassed several wooded chests of coins, jewels, and rarities of the region. These moderate riches would have gone far as Richard and Will joined the extended Wirral family on their new lands in England. It was on the last night's camp before boarding boats to Italy, which I caused something extraordinary happened.

"Will marched with his companions in his now familiar gloom. He saw or at least noticed very little of the countryside he traversed and now seemed totally indifferent that he would be crossing into Italy and going to see Rome and possibly the Pontiff! Will ate and drank sparingly since his stomach was still rebelling at most foods. He did not join the after-dinner discussions about Rome and returning home but went to his tent and slumped down on the robes. Sleep came quickly as it always did—until tonight.

"Will tossed his robes to escape the sweltering heat in his bed. But there was no sweltering heat in the tent. He immediately became chilled as the ambient temperature in the tent was about fifty-five degrees. Will drew his robes around him and instantly broke into a sweat as if he were working under a noon day sun in July. He dropped his robes and began to cool. The cool felt refreshing, and Will again snuggled into his warm robes in search of sleep. This time, sleep came upon him and Will relaxed into the cocoon of slumber, furtively expecting the sleep of days before.

"Instead, Will found himself in a room of indeterminate size. There were gauzelike curtains hanging from a ceiling, yet Will could see no ceiling and these curtains were full of motion as if a wind was pushing them about. Everything was light gray. The floor, yet Will perceived no floor, was covered in a fine mist. It could almost be called a smoke, but it bore no form as smoke can assume. Will was about to subconsciously comment on this place when the room took on a rosy hue. A small wisp of smoke appeared in front of Will and began to expand. As the smoke expanded, it rose to about twenty feet above the floor (if one could call it a floor) and the figure of a man emerged above the smoke. The vision was blurry and refused to sharpen when the vision of the dream began to speak. Of course it was me!

"My 'dream' voice was deep, clear, powerful, and refused to be ignored. I asked who dared approach Amir Al-Braheem. Will, thinking this was only a nightmare (as the other crusaders had described), clearly and forcefully replied that he was William, son of Richard of Wirral. As Will finished speaking, my apparition of smoke began to take on more detail. I was at least twenty feet tall and humanoid from the waist up to a bald head. A belt of what appeared to be finest gold was around my waist and proved to be a dividing line between the manlike being and the vaporlike being. Will shielded his eyes as I began to glow, then shine, then glare like sunshine on a broadsword. Through all of this, Will felt no fear. Incredibly, he felt drawn to me, this unlikely demon. Will spoke again, asking the 'demon' to repeat his name. In his studies of the ancient texts regarding 'fallen angels,' it was always best to get the creature to say its name. The texts, however, never mentioned why this was good. I answered as if my voice came from a thunderclap and repeated that I was Amir Al-Braheem! The gray curtains of the room stood out horizontally as if in a fierce storm. Will inquired that with the name of Amir, I must be a Saracen demon. I was wonderfully patronizing as I answered in a most sarcastic tone that I was neither Saracen nor demon. Amir was the name given to by the ancient scribes of Solomon but that 'the boy' may address me as commander if he wished. Will replied in his most humble tone that his wish was not to be called boy but to be addressed as Will. He also replied that he much preferred 'commander' over Amir! In truth, so did I. Will continued that he must now establish what kind of demon the commander is! I began to shine and then glare as before so that Will had to shade his eyes. He felt a wind of scorching hot air blow him backward. The wind was so strong that Will lost his footing and went spiraling into the gray curtains. I thought this was enough for one night. We would continue tomorrow night. Then I, the enclosure, the gray curtains, and the boy blinked out. All in all, it was a magnificent performance!

"Will awoke with a jerk as if yanked back to consciousness by an unseen cord. He was hot and sweating profusely. He must have cried out because several members of the band came to see if he needed assistance. His friends were astonished to see Will wet with sweat on such a cool night. One wondered out loud that Will must have been feverishly ill. As the sweat began to evaporate from his body and robes, Will started to shake with the cold and his friends helped him change into dry robes and dry bedding.

"Will thanked his companions and told them of the strange dream. All were amazed! All had encountered an apparition as Will had described in nightmares suffered when they first started the trip home. But in his companion's dreams, the demon never spoke or answered when spoken to. They also described a palpable terror during the dream, yet Will had no feelings of fear. What all of this could mean was on the minds of Will's friends as they left for their own tents. Will settled into his dry and fresh robes in hope of sleep. He would like to dream of this demon again and perhaps learn more of his origins and purpose in invading the dreams of him and his friends.

"As Will turned away from the tent entrance and relaxed on to the cool bedding, he noticed the box made of Palestine oak and a gift from Father Joseph begin to glow warmly. He would investigate tomorrow. The last thought before sleep overtook him was *Commander.* I heard him clearly!

"The next day was full of packing supplies and animals onto boats that would take them across the Adriatic Sea and into Italy. Most in the party were more than relieved to leave Byzantium and set foot on the European continent. The weather was overcast and windy, signaling the possibility of storms as the boat masters carefully studied the skies, waves, and spiraling seabirds for hints as to what might be in store for the two-hour excursion. It was finally agreed around midday that the trip would begin and that any weather would be within the design and capacities of the vessels to handle. Once away from the dock, the sails of each boat filled with a fresh wind and the tillers steered toward Brindisi.

"The boats sailed close to one another in order to assist any boat that may need assistance, and the passengers waved and shouted to each other as Byzantium faded away and the Adriatic became their only view. None of the crusaders, men-at-arms, or others in the party were sailors, and many quickly succumbed to the rolling and pitching boats by spewing the contents of their stomachs into the sea. The boat masters and seamen laughed and urged the passengers to focus their sight on a distant cloud to settle their uneasy balance and stomachs.

"Will was unaffected by the movement of the sea. His morning meal was intact and digesting nicely. He gazed off into the distance, seemingly focused on a point far out in front of the boats. His friends and fellow travelers commented to each other that Will seemed transfixed and almost apoplectic in the face of the churning seas. In Will's mind, the seas were mild and the winds comforting. He did not feel the roll and pitch of the boat or suffer any loss of balance. In his left hand, Will clutched the small box of Palestine oak and stared forward. The box was warm! The box was comforting! Then Will raised his right arm and shouted one word: 'Italy!'

"The boat masters skillfully docked the boats at the port and watched humorously as the passengers scurried ashore as quickly as possible. Several were still ashen in complexion and not looking well, but all set to the task of unloading the boats of animals and bundles. The boat masters were thanked and paid for the successful voyage and the party moved inland to search for a place to set up camp. They would seek out fresh supplies and water for the overland journey to Rome. It was also decided that the party would spend several days in place to resupply and allow all to recover from the voyage. Sighs of relief were heard all around.

Nine

Can I Help?
Road to Rome, March 1101

> *Narrator's note: Amir's recollection of Will and their meeting continues and Amir adds his reactions.*

"When Will awoke the next day, he became conscious of the fact that he felt good! His depression at losing his father was not gone but tempered with a curiosity about his dream and the gift from Father Joseph. His guilt at the decapitation of the young girl was also fading. Lessons had been learned and life was for the living! He arose and immediately joined his companions for the morning meal before setting out on the road to Rome.

"Many of his friends and companions remarked on how Will looked rested, even after the most horrible of nightmares. For his part, Will felt energized and focused on the road to Rome. After all, there were ancient scrolls and manuscripts to be read and translated. Spoils and booty raided from the Saracen institutions would add greatly to Will's understanding of the ancient world and the wisdom it held for the present and future generations. His father would want him to pursue this knowledge just as he had pursued the knowledge at the abbey of Father Joseph.

"The days were sunny and the nights were usually mild in this area of Salerno. Travel on the old Roman roads would be much easier than on the camel and goat paths of Palestine, and the travelers hoped for a quick and uneventful journey to Rome. It would be in Rome that final plans for the return to France and finally England would be made. Will hoped to have some time exploring at St. Peter's Basilica, maybe to search through ancient scrolls and manuscripts brought back from the Holy Land by early returning crusaders.

"But tonight, he wanted to dream of the 'commander.' Will was almost positive of my identity and of what I was capable of doing. Still, Will felt no fear. He did think that caution was the better path forward with me if indeed there was any path forward. He was impatient for the night to come in hopes of a conversation with the twenty-foot-tall man of fire. At the evening meal, Will ate ravenously wondering where this newly found appetite had arisen. When satiated, Will arose from the campfire and bid his friends a good evening. He would take a walk to clear his head and maybe even aid his digestion before retiring for the night.

"The night was moonless and the stars lit up the sky in their uncountable numbers. The air was cool and refreshing as Will finished his walk and returned to his tent. As he reclined on his bedding, Will grasped the small, wooden gift from Father Joseph. It was cool to the touch.

"He closed his eyes and uttered the one word aloud that seemed most appropriate to summon the being or perhaps have the being summon him: 'Commander!' In an instant, the box glowed hot and Will went utterly limp. He had the feeling of being pulled along in a vortex until he opened his eyes to find himself alone in the dull, gray room of curtains. This time, all Will did was imagine the word *commander* and a wisp of gray smoke began to rise from what he perceived as the floor of the room. The column of smoke thickened and became whiter as it grew taller. As the white smoke rose to about twenty feet, my outline of a humanoid began to form and take shape. Will marveled at my dark eyes, seeming without pupils, and the colored sparks that appeared on my fierce visage. I bore no hair.

"Heavily muscled shoulders and arms took shape along with a thick and powerful neck. Thin lips became apparent as my wide mouth became visible, upturned in what could be described as a maniacal grin. As the thin lips parted slightly, Will could see four, long, white canine teeth among two layers of sharp incisors. I then began to shine so brightly that Will had to shield his eyes. I was silent and altogether terrifying to behold. Will spoke first, addressing the being as 'lord commander,' and asked permission to speak.

"I was slightly startled as this son of Adam showed the proper respect and deference to one such as me. I nodded slightly, giving Will the permission he desired. His first question was to ask if he was in the presence of Amir Al-Braheem of the jinn. I remember feigning anger as my forehead wrinkled and my eyes became slits, sparking wildly. I leaned toward Will in a threatening posture, but he did not move. Will spoke again, telling he had read legends and stories of the jinn and the commander in his studies with Father Joseph and later with Fahad of the caravan. Will told me that it was an honor to actually be in the presence of one who had 'commanded the multitudes.'

"I drew back from my threatening posture and my lips, sneer, and canines softened and appeared less terrifying. Will noticed that I did not shine as brightly as before, and he no longer needed to shield his eyes. Will asked if it was I who had saved him from certain death at the hands of the robbers. Without waiting for an answer, Will asked if it was I who mitigated his grief and guilt at the death of his father and beheading of the child bandit. Was it I who steadied his balance and stomach during the voyage from Byzantium? Again without waiting for an answer, he asked me if he, a mortal man, could help the mighty Amir Al-Braheem. I was astounded!

"At this, my appearance changed drastically. The smoke drifted down as did my 'body' until it reached about seven feet in height. As the smoke faded, I took on an entirely human form with legs and hair. I was dressed in splendid silk robes slightly opened at the chest. I wore a ceremonial, scimitarlike sword at my waist. My facial features softened, and I took the form of an incredibly handsome man (if I do say myself)—perhaps of Persian descent. I finally spoke. I spoke in the tones of a man of power and position but did not try to intimidate. I told Will that in my thousands of years of existence, I had not needed or asked for any help from any entity. Will answered that he thought this time was different and that perhaps he could do a service that would please the commander. Again Will asked could he help.

"I spoke again and asked, 'Can you free me?'

"I told Will how I had offended the Most High when Lucifer and other angels and jinn were cast out. I told Will about being cast into servitude in King Solomon's palace then finally imprisoned in the small box for over two thousand years. I spoke of the vengeance and rage that had consumed me but how I felt a modicum of respect and even tranquility traveling in Will's presence. Will could hardly take all of the information in as I continued my tale. I spoke of rage and anger but how these powerful emotions were powerless to free me. Will asked how it was that a small, wooden box could contain one such as me.

"I explained that certain phytochemicals in the oak box essentially had the power to hold me inside. I also explained how unlike jinn imprisoned in brass lamps of legend could be freed by opening the stopper, I was imprisoned by Solomon himself. I feared that a simple opening of the box or its destruction at the hands of man would have the catastrophic event of annihilation and nonexistence for me.

"'There must be some sequence of events or rites to perform before the oak will release me,' I said.

"It was Will who spoke next, and he spoke of Rome and the scrolls of antiquity that may hold a clue to my release. Will vowed to the commander that he would search the ancient scrolls and texts brought back from the Holy Lands and find the answer to my imprisonment and ultimately my release. For this service, Will asked for one request be fulfilled. Amir sniffed and thought he may have misjudged the boy who evidently was seeking riches from the jinn as payback for freedom. I began to grow taller, brighter, and more foreboding as Will asked that his comrades and fellow travelers be blessed with pleasant dreams and fulfilling sleep.

"I was caught quite off guard by the simple and unselfish request and nodded in agreement as Will found himself pulled back into the vortex as before then waking on his bedding refreshed as if he had slept the entire night.

"Upon rising the next day, all of Will's traveling companions, crusaders, men-at-arms, and tradesmen alike remarked on the night's repose and lack of recurring nightmares. Perhaps they had shed whatever demon had followed them from the Holy Land. Will remarked that he thought so as well!"

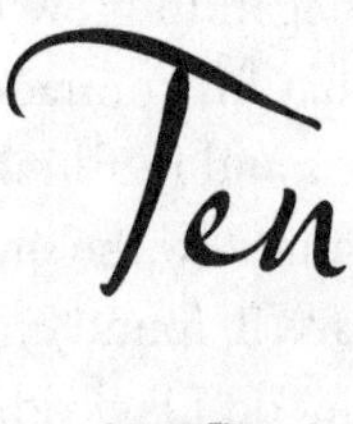

Ten

The Scrolls
Rome, spring 1101

"It was an achievement for Will to wait for the day's travel to end and turn into night. He desired nothing more than to converse with 'the commander,' question me, and learn from me! Ancient scrolls and manuscripts were one thing, but an authentic spirit of antiquity was almost too much for him to grasp. He regarded this like having a conversation with an archangel, such as Gabriel or Michael (poor comparison in my opinion). To Will, this creature had been created with the angels and Adam, the father of mankind. Will wished for sleep all through the day in order to be in touch with this altogether wonderful being: me!

"For my part, I was amused at Will's obsession but also prideful that any son of Adam would hold me in such regard. I was also ready to reveal to Will that we could communicate at any time, not just during Will's slumber. I would not reveal this to just any of mankind, but Will intrigued me. I knew I could teach Will much, but also I could learn much from the boy. Telepathy could be tricky with humans. Their small minds would quickly overload with the speed of thought and even damage to their consciousness could occur. I would need to take care with Will. I wished no harm to the boy as a result of my actions. I had also begun to trust that Will would find a way to free me.

"That morning, as the road to Rome stretched before them, Will was absentmindedly walking with his fellow travelers, wishing it were night, when a massive sound exploded through his head. Will put his hands to his ears and fell to his knees in agony. In an instant, the sound and pain were gone. Will's friends rushed to him and helped him to his feet. They asked what had happened to drop him to the ground in such pain. Will asked if they heard it. All of Will's friends looked at one another quizzically. Will quickly rose with his friend's assistance and looked at them in amazement! He questioned his friends again about the sound and how they did not hear it. No one had heard anything out of the ordinary. Will thanked his friends for their assistance but glanced over his shoulder as if to find the source of this sound only he could hear. There was nothing but the road over which they had trod.

"I nodded knowingly and drastically lowered the power of my thought to Will. His eyes widened as the unseen voice said his name. 'Will!' He started to answer the voice, but I interrupted and told him not to speak using voice and tongue but to slowly think the words he wanted to use in this communication.

"Will slowly thought out each word. 'Is—this—the—commander?'

"I was amused at the deathly pace of Will's thoughts and telepathically communicated that he would take all day to complete a sentence if this pace continued. I instructed Will, in a now well-modulated thought and normal speed of human thought, to simply *think* what he wanted to say and *think* it in a normal speed as if he were talking to someone. He understood this new and intriguing way of communication very quickly (for a human, I thought). I also warned Will that he must not appear to be communicating to the atmosphere or he would surely be labeled as mentally ill or—worse—possessed.

"And so it went for several days (and nights) with me instructing Will on telepathic communication and Will absorbing all that 'the commander' would relate. By the end of a fortnight, I was ready to communicate my presence, powers, and wishes to the human. Will, for his part, was ready to question and learn from this being of antiquity. I knew he wondered what secrets untold in Holy Scriptures, what knowledge of the Most High, and what destinies lay before them both.

"Amir told Will that he was a being essentially composed of energy. With concepts of matter and energy not well established, Amir likened himself to a flame but that he could 'solidify' in some instances for short periods of time. He also told Will that he could focus his being into something like lightning and travel great distances at great speeds—if he were free. Will asked about Amir's immortality and whether Amir suffered sickness and disease as did mankind. Amir explained that his energy, therefore his immortality, came from the common elements in the air and ground and that as long as there was an earth, he would exist. Amir continued that no jinn had ever suffered from sickness or disease because of the nature of their being: that of fire!

"The road to Rome seemed much less tedious to Will as I telepathically explained my beginnings, history, and ultimately imprisonment. Will learned that the jinn were created at the same time as the angels were created from light, mankind created from clay, and the jinn from fire. The angels were messengers of the Most High. They were immortal and possessing of great power over all that resided near the most High. Angels were protectors and advocates of all in existence as they related to the Most High. Some angels were so powerful they wanted to set their mansions and influence above the Most High and were cast out of the most perfect communion. Some jinn were caught up in this war and were also cast into the depths with Lucifer and the fallen angels. But some jinn stayed apart from the struggle but lost the favor of the Most High and ended up in a parallel existence, unable to interact with angels, humans, or devils. Of these few jinn, all were imprisoned by King

Solomon in vessels of brass and wood to search out, over the eons, to what purpose they were created.

"Will explained the call of the Crusades. Much of the land and individual holy sites had been taken over by the Saracen hordes. Since the seventh century, the lands and sites had been ruled by califs and rulers who understood the call of these lands to the faithful. Christians were welcomed and protected by no less than the Holy Book of Mohammed: the Koran. But lately, the rulers of the Holy Land had become more parochial and demanded that Christians deny their faith and convert to Islam. Pilgrimages and pilgrims had been attacked, holy sites had been razed, and the faithful had been slaughtered. Will told of how the leaders of the Eastern and Roman churches had called upon knights and men-at-arms throughout Europe to engage in a holy Crusade to recapture these sites and preserve them from the followers of Mohammed. Will asked me if I knew about Jesus the Christ, who had been sent to earth to reconcile mankind to the Most High and to forgive sins as the Son of God. I told him I was familiar with the one called Emmanuel but that He was sent to reconcile mankind to God. The jinn were not part of His mission on earth. The jinn had no savior sent from the Most High but were condemned to an existence separated from God and searching for a purpose under heaven. Will admitted that he knew nothing about the destiny of the jinn or Amir but that such a creature, created by the Most High, must have an enormous purpose and destiny to fulfill. Amir was a creature of fire, possessing powers and wisdom far in advance of the sons of Adam. There *must* be a destiny and reason for the existence of the jinn and Amir, the commander of the multitude!"

"True, I thought! *But what destiny?*

"The group reached Rome in midspring and immediately set out to have audience with the Holy Father. Will explained this was required of all returning crusaders so that the pope could assess the situation in the Holy Lands and order appropriate actions by the faithful. It was also a time to fulfill the promise of absolution of all sins, past and present, and to reward those who participated in the Crusades with loot and booty returned by earlier crusaders. Will sought out an Order of Scholastic monks with the hopes of finding scrolls or texts that may refer to the jinn in general and Amir specifically. After gaining entrance to the order, Will was introduced to a monk named Father John. Father John was of Nordic descent, probably Norwegian. He stood six feet, ten inches tall with a blond beard flowing to his waist. His eyes were a fierce blue as was Will's, and he stood as if a wooden rod were placed in his back. He had a wide mouth and a large grin filled with shining white teeth (not so common in the age). When Father John spoke, it reminded Will of my deep and resonate baritone. The monk asked Will to enter his cell in the monastery, within the Basilica of St. Peter.

"Will spoke in Latin and told Father John that he had studied with Scholastic monks in the Holy Land and had read and translated many scrolls and ancient texts. Will continued that he had become interested in an ancient race of beings called the jinn and asked if Father John was aware of any writings on that subject. A frown appeared on Father John's face, and he rose from his seat, stretching out the entire six feet, ten inches of his frame. He questioned if Will had encountered such a being in the Holy Land. Will did not speak immediately, and Father John issued a warning that in his studies of the legends of the jinn, no good came from their interaction. He had heard stories of jinn being released from their captivity in brass lamps only to destroy the one who freed them. Father John continued that in one scroll brought from Jerusalem by a returning merchant and attributed to one of Solomon's own scribes held the actual curse used by Solomon to imprison this unholy race of creatures. Father John looked down at Will and told him that his fear was that hidden within the scroll may be a key to unlock all jinn from their imprisonment. Will's excitement at the existence of such a scroll was almost unbearable. Had I wanted Will's death, why had I intervened and saved his life? Why had he soothed the fever of a small and very sick little girl?

"Will rose from his seat, looked directly into Father John's eyes, and lied that he had never encountered such a being and considered them to be a legend of Islam meant to bring nightmares to naughty children. Father John turned and walked to a brass box shaped somewhat like a casket, opened it, and retrieved its contents: two scrolls. He handed the obviously ancient documents over to Will and said for Will to take it from Rome, far away from Rome, and then burn them. Will's hands shook as he took possession of the scrolls. He thanked and reassured Father John that he would do what the monk asked.

Eleven

The Words of Solomon
Rome, spring 1101

> *Narrator's note: Dear reader, please remember that Amir in his box prison is always at Will's side and completely aware of what is occurring around them.*

"Will moved swiftly through the streets of Rome toward his encampment outside the city. Guilt from the lies he'd told Father John was building quickly, but it was counterbalanced by the potential contents of the scrolls. As Will passed the city gates, a thought in the clear, controlled, telepathic manner he had learned from Amir issued from his brain. He called to 'the commander.'

"I answered, and Will blurted out the events that had occurred with Father John and how he now possessed the scrolls that could unlock the curse of Solomon and ultimately free me. But I interrupted Will's story with the fact that I was fully aware of Will's interaction with Father John—just as I had been aware of Will's situation at the hands of the bandits. I told Will that as long as the small box of Palestine oak was carried by him, I could interpret situations through Will's senses. I think this was both reassuring and disturbing to Will. Before Will could think another thought, my voice filled his head and said that the two of them had established a very strong mind link, and so that Will did not feel possessed by me, he would break the mind link, reestablishing it only when both agreed.

"I snorted (in thought form) that although I was fond of Will as one is fond of a pet, I did not desire a twenty-four-hour-a-day conversation. At this, Will laughed audibly and freely as he spoke out loud that he agreed and would bow to 'the commander's' wisdom. For an instant and only an instant, a smile formed on my face. I could not recall the last time that had occurred.

"It was early in the afternoon when Will returned to the encampment. Many of his fellow travelers and families were still inside the city gates to sample foods and spices that were more familiar than in the lands of the east. Before starting his examination of the scrolls, Will called to me and asked if I wished to be with Will's thoughts as he worked. I agreed and felt an unknown sensation, which Will described to me as excitement! He immediately examined the scrolls. One was very old and written on papyrus, which would have been widely available in Solomon's times. The language appeared to be Egyptian, which also would have been spoken in Solomon's court (along with Syriac and several other Canaanite languages). The second scroll was constructed of fine paper typically used by monks in their restorations and translations.

"Will laughed aloud when he realized that the second scroll (written in Latin) was a word-for-word translation from the original Egyptian. Only certain items had not been translated, probably due to a defect or damage to the original scroll. Will scanned the translation scroll for words and phrases that were attributable to Solomon himself. Scribes of the times tried their best to capture every word of the speaker, especially if it was the king. The scribes also dared not ask the king to repeat a word or phrase, so each used certain symbols as a kind of code readable only by that scribe. These symbols could be extraordinarily difficult to translate, and they, along with defects or damage to the original scroll, led to a less than perfect rendition of the original. About one-fourth of the way through the scroll, Will found what he was looking for.

"Those words were 'So sayeth our Lord King Solomon.' Will's hand began to tremble as he realized that what was to be read next were the words of King Solomon himself, written down at the precise moment they were spoken.

"Solomon's words continued. 'The Lord God, Father and Most High, has given me absolute power over all jinn who were not cast out of heaven with Lucifer and the other fallen. Gabriel, messenger of the Most High, delivered unto me this ring with a central ruby stone symbolizing that power that I now exercise. My decree is that all jinn dwell in a parallel place, unseen and unrecognized by mankind. This place is neither heaven nor hell, but from here, there will be no encounters between the sons of Adam and the jinn, and there will be no escape. At the end of days, when all creation must be reconciled to the Most High, the jinn will be received in heaven and called keepers of everlasting flames. The commander of these jinn will not accompany his brothers to the parallel world. The commander of the jinn will remain in this world but be bound in a small vessel. He will remain in the vessel until he can reconcile himself to the Most High. He must search through the ages to find what it is he must do to be granted reconciliation. If through his powers the jinn attempts to escape this vessel, or enables any of mankind to assist him, he will immediately be swept to the parallel world with the rest of his brothers to await the favor of the Most High. However, if the commander ascertains the will of the Most High and seeks to reconcile, he will be freed to live among the sons of Adam as long as he wishes. His brother jinn will immediately be welcomed into heaven and be reconciled to the Most High.'

"The translation ended at this point with several symbols and potential words missing from both scrolls. My thoughts began to flow, and Will struggled to keep up. I recalled that I not only commanded the jinn at one time but also was responsible for their ultimate destiny. I had no idea at the time what it would take to reconcile with the Most High. I could receive no help, and if I tried to escape, I would suffer the same fate as my brothers in the parallel world: waiting. Feelings swirled of my old friends and allies and began to increase in intensity. Fury, rage, hate, and indifference filled my thoughts, and it was then that Will screamed in agony, fell to the ground, and grew damp with his own blood as it issued from his eyes, ears, nose, and mouth. I immediately broke the mind link, but Will was injured badly."

> *Narrator's note: It is noteworthy to add here that Amir's visage had grown dark and troubled as if he were reliving the event.*

Twelve

An Evil Is upon Us

The Road north of Rome, spring 1101

"While preparing for the day's march out of Rome, Will's friends noticed that his tent was still pitched and his belongings were not packed for the trip to the Alps. They called to him, and upon not being answered, they entered his tent to find Will close to death. Blood issued from all orifices of his head. He was unconscious, barely breathing, and had turned a hideous shade of blue. A healer was called to attend to Will, but when the poor man arrived and surveyed Will's condition, he turned and fled the tent, screaming about possession and evil spirits. One of Will's friends noticed that the bleeding was lessening and pulled Will into his arms. He screamed Will's name and shook him as to awaken him from some horrible nightmare. Will drew in a deep breath, then another as his color began to return. His companions cleaned his head of the viscous and dried blood, bound him in clean robes, and lay him upon his bedding. They noticed the two scrolls on the ground and retrieved them, placing them in a leather skin until Will regained consciousness. They also placed Will's leather belt and pouch in his hands as they knew he treasured the box of Palestine oak within. Two of Will's friends decided that the larger party should leave for the Alps ahead of them and that they would attend to their friend for a few days then catch up with the group before they reached the Alps. The knights and crusaders agreed (although reluctantly) to the plan and set out to the north on the next dawn.

"I was in a catatonic state! My mighty and indefatigable self-image was shattered. My strength of purpose and iron will were wholly decimated. I thought I had destroyed my only link to mankind and now was utterly alone. In a moment of rage, had I obliterated the mind of the only companion I had known for over two thousand years? In that instant, I realized why the jinn were held apart from the sons of Adam. It became apparent that the jinn were altogether too powerful to coexist with humans. As the angels were separated from humans, so should the jinn. Then what was the destiny of his race? Why had they been created by the Most High if there was no purpose? Questions and more questions poured through my mind. Purpose and destiny of the jinn were mine to determine? I thought that the Most High was cruel to lay this burden upon me alone. More and more blasphemous thoughts appeared and disappeared in my mind as the rage increased.

"It was this precise moment when I was most distraught that a small, weak thought came to my mind. 'Commander, are you there?'

"I moved quickly to gain control of his mind and the stream of thoughts and emotions racing through his consciousness to reestablish the mind link. In a calm, controlled, and almost consoling manner, I answered Will that I was with his thoughts. Will asked me what had happened. Why had he awakened on his bedding robes, and why was there blood on his face and clothes? Will told me of remembering translating the scroll and being linked to my thoughts and then a feeling like his head exploded!

"I slowly and calmly told Will how the translation of the scroll had left little hope of escape or freedom from the oak box. I continued that the rage and anger that had accompanied me through the millennia surged in my mind. This surge of the most negative and hurtful thoughts and emotions had overwhelmed Will and almost destroyed his consciousness. He interrupted that thanks were due to me for breaking the mind link and saving his life. Will then sensed a profound sadness in my thoughts and called out loud for 'the commander' to brighten his mood. I, in an element of regret never before felt, told Will that it was my fault that he lay injured and bloodied. It was me, Amir of the jinn, commander of the multitude, who almost destroyed the only connection to mankind and to the only being in thousands of years who put my welfare above his own.

"Will's only answer was 'Help me heal.'

"I was taken aback by this request since I was certainly no master of healing arts for mankind and the jinn were never ill.

"Will answered that through his studies of the ancient healers and philosophers, the mind (which had always been thought of separately from the body) and body were intricately connected and that for true healing to take place, both aspects of the person must be treated. Will continued that because Amir is a creature of energy and never damaged or ill, that energy must have healing and protective qualities as do certain herbs and other botanicals. Will said that he was quite positive that my intervention of pleasant dreams with the girl Benazir hastened her healing along with the ministrations Will provided.

"I was skeptical but intrigued that I may possess healing powers along with my obvious and formidable destructive powers and asked Will what was I to do to aid in his recovery. Will asked me through the mind link to clear all thoughts except those of healing from his brain. Will then took the small oak box out of its pouch and held it with his bare hand. Will asked me to allow a tiny fraction of my energy to pass through the box and into his hand. I agreed that the flow of energy must be slow and well contained so as not to do more damage. Will asked one more thing of me, and that was for sleep as the process of healing took place. He no sooner finished the thought than his eyes grew heavy, fluttered, and closed.

"Will's remaining friends checked in on him throughout the night but always found Will sleeping soundly and looking comfortable.

As the sun arose on the following morning, Will's friends returned to his tent only to stop in amazement as Will greeted them, dressed and ready for the day's travel. An astonished companion remarked that yesterday he seemed at death's door only to rise this morning looking as if he had seen heaven's gates! Will's other companions backed slowly away, not quite believing what stood before them. Perhaps he was possessed as the healer had screamed out yesterday as he ran away from Will's presence. Will laughed heartily and said he had reserved some special herbs and elixirs from Father Joseph in the abbey and it was those that had cured him, not possession and certainly not evil possession. Will asked his friends to move out and travel quickly in order to catch up with the main party. They agreed and caught up with their traveling companions in a single day. All were amazed at Will's recovery and told of how they prayed for him and that the Christ would restore him to them. Will smiled and thanked *all* parties that brought him back, both in heaven and earth. Then Will murmured so as not to be heard as he thanked a jinn in a little oak box."

Thirteen

A Practice of Healing
The Italian Alps, late spring 1101

> *Narrator's note: As Amir tells the story of his growing relationship with Will, his visage changes again to a lighter expression and ease of communication.*

"It was late May when the returning crusaders and their fellow travelers marched into one of several passes that would take them through the Alps and into France. Their timing had been good and most of the passes were clear of snow and ice with only the peaks and summits retaining the white, winter's covering. Some of the travelers wondered aloud if these might be the same passes employed by Hannibal in the third century as he sought to invade Rome with his elephants.

"Their trip had been uneventful and even exciting at times when they would pass travelers going toward Rome and beyond; trading food and other items and telling stories about their journeys helped break the day-to-day monotony of the road. The temperatures were warm enough during sunlight to shed the heavier robes for lighter clothing, but a roaring fire and warm bedding was necessary to break the chill of evenings. Will and I formed the mind link almost every day to discuss the scrolls, parts of which Will had been unable to translate. I also was keenly interested in exactly how he had healed of the damage he had done to Will.

"The animals brought on this journey were the original horses, oxen, cattle, and sheep, less those used for food or that died naturally or at the canines of predators. Many had bred to produce young, and all were necessary in their nature for the returning crusaders. One knight had bred his huge and powerful draft stallion to an Arabian mare captured in battle. The resulting foal was large, powerful, and potentially faster than any horse known in Europe at the time. The knight was delighted with this foal and was determined to start a breeding farm when he returned to his lands near Claremont in France.

"It was this knight who approached Will one evening and asked to speak with the healer/blacksmith. Will kneeled in respect to the noble and addressed him as 'my lord.' The knight told Will to rise and listen to the story of his foal. Will was aware of the horse but had not shod it as he had its sire and mare. The knight continued that he feared the foal was becoming lame. It did not run and jump with the joys of youth as it had done earlier. The foal seemed content to follow its mother at a slow pace and even then appeared to limp, carrying the right hind leg aloft as it walked. The knight had seen this lameness in other foals that ended up being humanely destroyed.

"The crusader, obviously distraught, asked Will to examine his foal and restore it to health if that was possible. Will admitted that he too had witnessed the lameness described by the crusader in other young horses and it was almost always fatal and painful if the horse was not destroyed before the lameness progressed too far. The hard eyes of the crusader were glistening and tearing as he asked Will to attempt to treat his young horse. Will agreed and asked the knight to bring the horse to his tent as soon as possible so as not to let the lameness claim any more of the leg.

"The knight returned within minutes with the foal and its mother. Will told the knight to leave the horses with him overnight and he would attempt to treat the advancing lameness. The knight thanked Will, turned, and walked back to his encampment. The foal was skittish and whinnied in fear as Will attempted to stroke its mane. Speaking gently as he had done to so many horses in the past, Will pulled the rope around the foal's neck slowly toward him. Will's touch was reassuring and calming to the foal, and he led it in taking a few steps. The right hind leg came up and was not lowered for any more steps. Continuing to speak slowly and calmly, Will reached down to feel the hoof and lower bones of the foal's damaged leg. It was hot with inflammation, swelling quickly and obviously painful to the foal. He walked the horse over to a hay wagon and dumped a large amount on the ground. Will gently pulled the horse down to the hay bed and off of the damaged hoof. The young horse did not object.

"He called out for a friend to gather several of his shirts and soak them in cold water before bringing them to the hay bed. The air was cool, and as the cold water on the shirts evaporated, they grew even cooler. Will called to his friend again to go to the north-facing rock outcropping about one hundred yards ahead and gather a basketful of remaining winter's snow. When the friend returned, Will applied the snow to the shirt bandages, and he could feel the foal relax as the cold took away the pain. Will thanked his friend and bid him good night.

"I called out first to Will, asking to establish the mind link. I, in my best impression of smugness, asked Will if he would require assistance in treating the animal. Will replied that if he could get the inflammation down and the horse off its feet for a few days, he thought the animal would recover. Then Will would apply a special shoe to the injured hoof to cushion and protect it even further before regular horseshoes were used. I sniffed loudly that I was pleased that Will could handle this himself. A broad grin traversed Will's face as he told me he would like to 'test' my powers of healing.

"Again I sniffed loudly and in apparent incredulity that Will would even suggest such a thing as a test! Had it not been me,

Amir, who restored Will from his injury? Will agreed that it was indeed true but that it was also true that I had inflicted those injuries! Will could feel my spirit begin to falter and pressed the conversation forward. 'Commander,' Will called out loudly and was immediately answered, 'I am with your thoughts.' He told me that his test was not one to confirm that which was already known and that I was an extraordinarily powerful creature. But to determine how finely I could channel these powers toward a desired outcome. I was intrigued and again flattered that this human would place my development in such high regard. Will continued and laid out his plan for my test and the treatment plan for the foal. I remember asking if the two plans intersected and was assured that they did.

"Will outlined his plan to me. First, he wanted to know if I could keep the horse asleep and off its feet for three days. Perhaps I could provide some pleasant dreams for the foal to keep it tranquil. I laughed, but the laugh was one of aloofness as I asked just what a foal would dream. Will continued that all the foal knew in his young life was his mother, nursing, and the grassy meadows it played in before reaching the Alps. Then Will wanted to try to pull the inflammation and possible infection out of the foal's hoof by reversing the process in which I provided healing energy to Will's injuries.

"To accomplish this, I would use Will's hand as conduit to draw energy out of the affected areas. The result would be a lessening of the inflammation and a lessening of the disease progression—potentially stopping or reversing it. I started to ask a very important question when Will interrupted his thoughts with assurances that the energy pulled away from the foal would not in any way harm me.

"That was not my question, but I agreed to the plan and said to begin. Will could feel my thoughts move toward and then into the little animal's brain. The foal trembled just once before its eyelids lowered and its breathing became slow and regular. Through the mind link, Will could see the projection I was sending to the sleeping foal. It was an endless, green pasture filled with every manner of tall grasses, flowers, and clover. In the distance was the mare beckoning her colt to come and nurse then gallop about this glorious playground. With his left hand, Will grasped the small oak box, and with his right hand, he gently massaged the affected leg and hoof.

"The foal had no reaction, but Will immediately was aware that his right hand was getting red, hot, and painful. The sensation was followed by the heat and pain traveling up Will's arm, across his back, and down to his left hand. As the extracted inflammation moved out of his left hand and into the oak box, Will's right hand returned to normal. I felt nothing. Will repeated this action two more times but then had to cease due to a pain buildup in his right hand.

"Sweat had broken out on his forehead even as the nighttime chill descended on him. His right hand was red and throbbing, but the sensation was slowly moving up his arm, across his back, down his left arm, then out of his body and into the box. He wiped the sweat away to get a look at the foal. It was resting peacefully with its legs and hooves quivering as if moving in a dream. The affected leg and hoof showed no sign of disease or injury, and Will sighed heavily. It had worked.

"For the next two days, the little horse slept soundly, rising only to nurse from the mare before returning to the hay wagon for a boost inward. On the third morning, the foal awoke and climbed out of the hay wagon, shaking itself thoroughly. It paid little attention to the new horseshoes that had been applied as it bounded over to the mare for breakfast. All in the encampment were amazed at the foal's recovery, and high praises were raised to Will. Some likened him to the healers of ancient times, while others teased him about becoming a "son of Merlin"!

"That same morning, the French knight and nobleman approached Will with an offer to join his household. The king would surely give Will a knighthood, and 'Sir William' could enjoy all the riches and privilege offered a nobleman. Will considered the wonderful offer briefly but told the knight that he must return to his kinsmen and the new family lands and holdings in England.

He thanked the knight for his offer and wished that the foal grew strong and fast.

"Will was about to turn away when the knight called out to him. As Will turned, the knight tossed a bag to him. The bag was unusually heavy, and when Will opened it, he understood why. It was filled with several pounds of gold coins! A gift from Sir Robert of the House of Normandy."

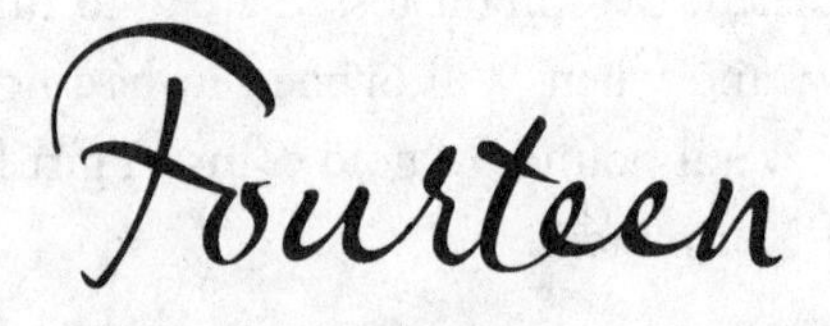

A Thief

Near Claremont, summer 1101

"As the travelers approached Claremont, many groups began to break away toward their individual homes. Will said his goodbyes to many friends and comrades of their adventures in the Holy Land and times upon the road. Strong relationships had been formed and would last for many years, even as knights and dukes challenged each other for land and power on both sides of the English Channel.

"There were also many new faces being encountered as traders and merchants swarmed the crusaders in search of rare treasures and Saracen wealth. It was late on a summer's day that Will left the merchants and crusaders' strange bazaar to return to his tent. He saw a small, fast stream close to the encampment and wanted to bathe and free himself of many days' worth of dust from the road. Will stripped down to a waistcloth and walked down toward the stream. As he lay down, the cool, fresh water plunged over his head and body as if he stood under a waterfall. His skin tingled and turned rosy with the chill as he swept his arms and hands through the clean waters, dislodging at least several pounds of dirt and dust from his body. The chill of the water finally convinced him to leave the stream and return to his tent for a robe.

"As he approached his tent, a friend called out asking about the coolness of the water in the stream. Will laughed and answered that it was perfect. That is when Will saw a small figure, like a child, scurrying away in desperate haste. Will dashed the remaining few yards to his tent and rushed inside to find all of his belongings strewn about and scattered throughout it. He evidently had interrupted the thief in the performance of his larceny and caused him to flee before completely ransacking Will's belongings.

"Will searched through the pile on the floor of his tent and unbelievably found the bag of gold coins. The tie around the bag had not been disturbed. Piece by piece, Will located most of his belongings when the most terrible of thoughts entered his mind. He could not find Amir's oak box, which was usually secured by a leather tie to his belt. The tie was on the ground, and the box was gone!

"A series of horrible thoughts flashed through Will's mind. What if the thief tried to open the box? What if, realizing it was only a box, the thief threw it away? What if Amir intervened? The last question filled Will with the most dread. Will knew that I was fully capable of rendering this thief/child's brain into a thin soup. Will stood erect and cleared his mind before calling out, 'Commander.' The expected reply of 'I am with your thoughts' did not materialize. He tried again and got the same result: silence! Will began to panic.

"At the same time, the thief/child was moving quickly and with great stealth through the encampment, across an open field, and into a small cavern. The entrance was partially blocked by rocks and tree limbs and could only be accessed by someone of small stature. Also, the cavern was off the main road and not close to any agricultural or pastoral activities so no one ever paid much attention to it. The thief/child made it his practice to enter or exit the cavern only by dark. In the six months he lived in the cavern, he was never discovered by the travelers on the road or servants working in a nobleman's fields several miles away. From this hideaway, he could raid the sleeping groups of travelers for food, clothing, and an occasional coin or two.

He disciplined himself to take only small amounts in his raids, and sometimes the travelers did not even realize anything was missing. He, however, was well-fed, clothed, and free.

"Over time as the amount of coins grew, he would walk to a small village outside of Claremont and purchase items, such as candles, needle and thread, a knife, meats, and the occasional piece of fruit. He felt he was doing quite well for himself—master of his surroundings and a slave to no one. The thief/child, once inside his cavern, lit a candle and settled down to examine tonight's plunder. It had been a close call when the one man returned to his tent from the bath in the stream. It was only the man's call to a friend that had warned him and allowed for an escape.

"Will ran through the encampment, calling to everyone that a thief was among them. All of the knights and men-at-arms drew swords and spears in response. A call went out to search the encampment and find the intruder. Darkness was quickly overtaking them as several lit torches to aid with the search, but after several minutes, it was apparent that the thief had escaped. As the men gathered back at the encampment, Sir Robert, whose young colt Will had saved, approached Will and asked what was missing.

"Had the intruder taken the bag of gold coins? If found, the knight promised a quick execution for the perpetrator. Will told Sir Robert that the gold was secure and on his person. But a small, wooden box, given to him by a monk in the Holy Land, was missing. Will did not tell Sir Robert about me but only that the box was an artifact from the temple of King Solomon so in a way, it was priceless. Again Sir Robert promised a quick execution but specifically mentioned burning at the stake! They would search again with tomorrow's light, but they would not have far to search.

"The thief/child accounted for his raid: one small loaf of wheat bread, a string of dried meat (probably deer), a small robe made from lamb's wool, a woman's scarf (he hoped it was silk), and a small, wooden box with a sealed lid. It was intriguing and the thief/child shook the box next to his ear, searching for a telltale rattle but found none. He had a passing thought about breaking open the box, but his hunger turned his thoughts to the wheat bread and dried meat.

"To make a most excellent feast, he withdrew a wine bottle from its enclosure and poured a generous amount into a cup. The wine was red and full of warmth as he ate the bread and meat. He had learned to enjoy wine and to respect its power. A quick memory of his first taste, which turned into a full bottle, which turned into a day and night of stomach upheavals and spinning surroundings, had taught him to limit the drink to one cupful.

"Having filled his innards with the bread and meat and a goodly portion of wine for one his size, the thief/child lay down on his bedding and fell asleep without delay. It was then that I engaged.

"I was and had been aware of the thievery going on in Will's tent yet chose to withhold any action until I understood the entire situation. As soon as the thief/child was asleep, I entered his dreams. At first, they were the dreams of a thief raiding and pillaging caravans but then moved to family and loss. The thief/child was about fourteen years old. He had been orphaned in a battle between dukes of Calais and Plymouth fighting for landfalls on each continent. His father, mother, and older sister had been killed as nobles fought nobles and peasants were sacrificed. He had grown hard and incorrigible against these nobles who cared less about the people who worked and slaved for them. As far as he was concerned, they could all die. He would rob them, steal from them, and eventually kill them if he could.

"His name was Benjamin, but he preferred the shortened version of Ben to the few people he could call friend. I studied the boy's thoughts for a moment and then set a stage for a drama to be played out. Immediately, Ben found himself in a courtroom, surrounded by travelers he had robbed in the past. His accuser was the man from the stream, and his judge was a terrible apparition: about twenty feet tall, bald, eyes with no pupils, seemingly composed of fire, huge canine teeth, and a horrible deep voice commanding that all be silent to hear the charges against the thief called Ben.

"Ben's accuser from the stream pointed a fleshless finger toward

Ben and uttered the word 'Him!' All in the courtroom stood and repeated the accuser's word 'Him!' The apparition began to change, and its lips peeled away, revealing rows and rows of sparkling teeth. The boy tried to look away, but his eyes were held in place by the dingy fingers of the apparition. He tried to scream, but his voice was silenced as all of the accusers reached out with bony hands to grip his throat. A final attempt to scream led to an unearthly voice spewing from his throat, calling on the boy to confess before death. Finally, a scream of terror escaped the boy's throat and he awoke, wet with sweat and trembling with fear. There would be no more sleep for him tonight.

"At the dawn, Ben stirred from his hideous night and shook himself mightily. Whatever demons had visited him the last evening were not welcomed back for another round. Ben resolved to find the man from the stream (probably a wizard) and return the box to him. He would beg forgiveness, blame his youthful age, and refer to his being orphaned in order to be released from the curse of the previous evening. I was pleased at instilling the fear and now would guide the installation of forgiveness and potential destiny."

> *Narrator's note: I stopped the recording and before Amir could object, I asked him why he would be interested in this boy's forgiveness and destiny. His response would foreshadow many of his human interactions to come. "I found him deserving of another chance."*

"Ben dressed himself in his ugliest of robes to add credence to his orphan story and proceeded toward the crusaders' encampment. At the edge of the encampment, he called out to the travelers that he was the thief who had raided their camp last night. Multiple men-at-arms and knights responded with weapons drawn and threats of disembodiment. Sir Robert had mounted his huge draft horse and looked to be all of fifteen feet tall as he approached the youth who had just dropped to his knees. Sir Robert called to Will, who emerged from his tent to behold this spectacle.

"Sir Robert thundered at the boy regarding any stolen items that may be in his possession. Ben produced the small oak box, which he handed to Will. Sir Robert thundered again about the severe penalties, even unto death, that await any who steal from God's warriors. Ben lowered his head in acceptance. During all this thundering from Sir Robert, his young colt had turned away from its mare. It approached the boy at a slow gallop, careening into him and knocking the thief/child, facedown into the ground. The foal raised his front legs and pawed at the air in front of thc boy. It danced about and lowered its head to nudge Ben, who was still trying to regain his feet. It knocked the boy down again, but there was a definite playfulness in the colt's actions. Ben leapt to his feet and shouted to the colt to stop, and the colt immediately stood still.

"Tentatively, Ben reached for the colt's head and stroked its mane as the young horse willfully stayed next to him, prancing and nudging Ben's shoulder. The thief/child's face broke into a wide grin. Will offered to Sir Robert that a bond such as this, established this early in a colt's life, was impressive and probably unbreakable and that he should consider Ben a potential custodian and trainer of this animal. Sir Robert could do nothing but agree, but he would know more of this boy/thief and how it came that he took on the role of highwayman and how he must establish trust with his equine charges.

"Ben interrupted, asking what proposal Sir Robert had envisioned. Sir Robert, looking ever so sternly, said he was proposing that Ben accompany him and his party to Normandy, where Ben would work with Sir Robert's livestock, especially horses, and see to their welfare and development. Ben blurted out that he would not be a servant or slave for anyone. Sir Robert thundered again that he did not offer positions to servants and slaves but to freemen and overseers. Ben dropped to one knee and immediately pledged fealty to Sir Robert and his heirs. Sir Robert told Ben to go and fetch his belongings because they would set course for Normandy tomorrow. Sir Robert turned and asked Will if he was satisfied with the arrangement, upon which Will agreed wholeheartedly. Later, after all were asleep in their tents, Will called out to me, 'Commander.' The familiar reply of 'I am with your thoughts' echoed through Will's mind. 'Commander, was it you who brought the thief/child back into our midst? Was it you who caused the young colt to attach itself to the boy?'

"My reply was simply 'Perhaps!'"

Fifteen

A Change in the Weather
Calais, late summer 1101

"The next day, everyone within the encampment joined together to wish Sir Robert and his party a joyful return to his castle and lands. Sir Robert had proven himself time and time again to be a brave and loyal crusader and friend. His group numbered twenty men-at-arms, several wives who had accompanied the group, and several children from infants to teenagers. Will mused that the entire group of travelers would be reduced by half. The former, formidable gathering of knights and their entourages was now looking a bit small and feeble. Sir Robert thundered (as he usually did) a series of hearty thanks and farewells to the rest of the travelers and turned his group toward home. Will saw the former thief/child leading the huge mare and its playful foal along with Sir Robert's party and raised a hand of farewell to young Ben.

"At this gesture, Ben turned and approached Will. He bowed his head toward Will and upon raising it met Will's fierce, blue Viking eyes. Ben asked Will outright if he was a wizard or some angel/demon come down to earth. Will laughed soothingly and answered that he was none of those but a blacksmith with some knowledge of languages. Ben questioned Will again. Was it he who put those awful dreams into his head two nights past? Again Will answered that he had no such power. Then Ben asked if Will was responsible for the events that were even now transforming his life and who he should thank. Will answered that perhaps there was an invisible spirit at work here, but he told Ben not to dwell on the unexplainable but delight in the destiny that appeared to be unfolding in front of him. Will admonished Ben to serve Sir Robert with dignity and integrity and to keep charge of his horses with love and compassion.

"Ben dropped to one knee and held an outstretched hand toward Will, who immediately grasped it, raising Ben to his feet. Ben asked why, when all the others in the encampment called loudly for his punishment, even his death, Will was kind and offered mercy. Will told Ben of being orphaned during the crusade and his feeling of being utterly alone. He told of the death of the young girl who had killed his father with a bolt from a crossbow and how it seemed to drain him of hope, compassion, and the joy that all life brings.

"He also told Ben of his quest for knowledge and love of ancient texts and scrolls and the treasures that lay within them. Will explained that he still was in search of his destiny and hoped he would be as fortunate as Ben in finding a new life's adventure and purpose. Ben threw his arms around Will and held him tightly for a brief moment. Upon releasing Will from his grasp, Ben uttered, 'We could be brothers.' Ben turned and, with the horses in tow, rejoined Sir Robert's party now headed home.

"The road led to Calais, where the remaining crusaders and parties would cross the channel to Dover on the island of Britannia. Arrangements had to be made for ferries to make the passage, and the weather had turned stormy. Even as Will and the others trudged north and west toward Calais in miserable rain and wind, they all held an anticipation of going home. It had been six years away from kinsmen, homelands, and all that used to be familiar. Several of the remaining young ones had never seen England, being born in the Holy Land. As they approached Calais and saw the sea in the distance, all became excited and joyful—even if wet and windblown. The group pitched their tents and made camp just a mile or so from the village.

"Calais was a fishing village with a natural harbor. Throughout history, the village had been used as a doorway to Britain. It was written that Julius Caesar had gathered hundreds of boats to get over eight thousand Roman soldiers across the channel to attack the island. It had been fought over and won, then lost, many times in the past but always seemed to thrive because of its strategic placement on the continent. When not besieged by one army or another, Calais was also an important trading post for raw goods like wool moving to mills in France and Flanders and finished goods like cloths and tools moving toward Plymouth and London. The ferry system always seemed to thrive as the movement of people and goods increased. Ferries could be hired at any time for any purpose except at times of foul weather. Foul was an accurate description of the weather on that day with high winds, heavy rains, and angry seas prevailing. Many a ferryman had seen his last day attempting a crossing on a day such as this. None would hire out until this weather cleared.

"On about the fourth foul weather day, Will stood up in his soggy tent, cleared his mind, and called out, 'Commander!' Immediately, Will's mind was filled with the sound of the mind link, 'I am with your thoughts.' Will casually asked me if I had any experience modifying the weather. I mused that he had never considered such a thing since the elements of wind, rain, snow, and storms had no effect on me. I did not feel cold or heat so was generally unconcerned with the weather. But Will pressed on, asking if I would consider the weather and if duly considered, could consciously modify it? I admitted that I could and had modified wind speed and direction in a relatively small area but had never been able to alter temperature except on a very limited space, like a room or other small enclosure.

"To demonstrate this, I lowered the temperature in the tent to the point where Will could see the condensation of his breath. Now wet and cold, Will asked me to return the warmth. I did so and added several extra degrees of heat to the point of bringing sweat to Will's skin. He thanked me for the unplanned demonstration but asked me to concentrate on the wind. Storms in this area typically came off the ocean, blowing from the southwest to the northeast. He asked if I could exert such a force on the wind so as to blow the storm away from Calais and the channel crossing. Again I told Will I had never considered such a thing but would attempt the feat as Will wished.

"Amir asked Will to take my box outside so that I could sense the wind speed and direction. Will threw a cover over his head and, holding my box tightly, stepped outside the tent. He was immediately met with a howling wind slapping a hard-driving, horizontal rain at his face. Will pulled the head cover down even lower as he outstretched his arm, holding the small box skyward. Will sensed warmth coming from the box that rapidly grew hot to the touch. Then, as quickly as the box had grown hot, it returned to its ambient temperature. Will withdrew his arm and the box in his hand and waited for something to happen. What happened next both frightened and thrilled Will.

"A flash of light illuminated the entire sky and a single lightning bolt crashed down, striking the ground near the harbor. The strike was strong enough to cause a small tremor in the ground at Will's feet, followed by the loudest crack of thunder he had ever experienced. For a moment, Will was blinded by the flash. As he regained his vision, Will caught glimpse of a monstrous waterspout spinning in the channel and moving northwest. Will saw it for only a moment as the watery cyclone picked up speed and then vanished over the horizon.

"Within minutes, the overcast began to break apart and the wind turned, now coming out of the southeast at a moderate pace. The sun broke free and shone brightly in a clearing blue sky. Will looked toward the harbor and the waters of the channel as they calmed and turned from the dull gray storm colors to a beautiful and inviting blue-green hue. Will stood there, outside, as others started to emerge from their tents and from down in the village. As the gentle wind and warming sun stroked Will's face, a thought from me popped into his head. 'Is this satisfactory?' Will replied, 'No, Commander. This is incredible!'"

Sixteen

An Alternative
Calais, late summer 1101

"As the weather cleared, knights from Britain moved down to the harbor to make the necessary arrangements to move the party across the channel and landing in Dover. Will had already offered to help pay for the ferry but was refused by the knights. Each said he and his father's service to them and their families for the last six years more than paid for a boat ride. As the knights were negotiating terms with the ferrymen, Will had returned to his tent—still in a state of amazement! He could feel my mind link and asked me exactly how I had so radically changed the weather.

"I explained that all jinn have varying amounts of power over the four elements: fire, water, earth, and air. I was always aware of these powers but had little use for them in the service of Solomon. The elements of water, air, and earth were mainly the province of mankind. A jinn could renew any elements he needed directly from the element of fire. Mankind's power over fire was rudimentary and interim at best. Will pushed me further for an answer on how I accomplished such a feat. I was feeling slightly annoyed at the questions but told Will that my mind had power over objects, visible or invisible and solid or vaporous. I could move them, manipulate them, and disrupt them. No jinn, however, could animate them. That power was reserved to the Most High. I continued that I could give energy to objects both animate and inanimate. Likewise, I could also take energy away. I explained that although I had these powers, I could no more explain how they operated than Will could explain how his mind formed a thought. Will asked if I would use these powers to be of service to mankind, to which I answered curtly, 'I have for you!'

"Will sensed that I was rapidly tiring of the question-and-answer dialogue and told me that some progress had occurred in the translation of the scroll from Solomon's temple. I was instantly interested and bombarded Will's head with an endless stream of questions at a staccato pace. Will's hands went to his head and a look of pain was taking shape when I realized Will's brain could process neither the speed nor the volume of my thoughts. I silenced this communication, and after a moment, when Will seemed recovered, I asked if Will would try again at a more normal pace for a human. He took a deep breath, exhaled slowly, and said he would continue.

"The progress in translating the scroll was that ancient Egyptian does not translate to Latin on a word-for-word basis. For example, in Egyptian, there are dozens of words that mean 'sand' in Latin. Will continued that a word in a certain passage kept translating as 'transfusion,' which rendered the passage meaningless to him. But another word in Latin made the passage meaningful. I pressed Will for the answer. He concluded that the passage was meant to read, 'The commander of the jinn shall be held to one *transference* in the eventuality that the original binding vessel become uninhabitable, thereby sweeping the commander to the parallel world of his brothers.' I demanded to know what the passage meant to him. Will told Amir that although he could not free the jinn, he could move him to another vessel. I remember being crushed. Freedom still eluded him, but a new jail was readily available if needed.

"Will interrupted my sarcastic thoughts and offered that 'what' and 'where' the commander could be transferred was not prescribed in the scroll so was within their power to decide both. I was still doubtful, but Will insisted that eventually I would reconcile with the Most High and find my purpose and destiny. But until then, would I rather be prisoner in a box or a palace? My mood lifted slightly at the prospect of a palatial prison at least until the Most High revealed what I must do to gain my ultimate freedom.

"In the meantime, the knights had returned to the much smaller encampment with news of the ferry arrangements. All would board in two days' time from the docks of ferryman Francis of Dunkirk. He was a Frank but was the most experienced ferryman available. He had four boats capable of transporting the entire party and was available immediately because the knights paid in gold! The two days passed without incident or portents of inclement weather. The entire group, complete with families and animals, proceeded to board one of Francis of Dunkirk's four boats. Will's blacksmith tools were loaded early, and he lingered on the docks as the others scrambled aboard. As he faced westward to Britain, the sun was warm upon his face and the breeze was mild. Will's thoughts were of his family and his uncles who had no knowledge of his father's death. Would he be greeted as his father's heir and a man, or as an orphan and youngster needing a trustee? Will called to his constant companion, 'Commander,' to which the mind link was secured and the answer came back, 'I am with your thoughts!' Will was about to ask rhetorically about his family in Wirral when he was interrupted by my thoughts. 'I suppose you will want calm seas.' Will laughed and replied, 'If you have no objection.'

"I did not."

Seventeen

The Road to London
Plymouth/London, early fall 1101

"The crossing was without incident and all were excited to make landfall on the coast of Britain. Plymouth was a seafaring town with a natural harbor and well-defined port. Francis of Dunkirk cursed the entire way across but did so in French so it sounded lovely. My promise of calm seas came true, and all disembarked without losing their stomachs even once! Upon landing on English soil, local constables surrounded the party, demanding to know the place of their origin and destination. After all, there were taxes to be paid and undesirables to be detained. Sir Harold of Nottingham explained that theirs was a party of crusaders returning from the Holy Land and under the protection of Pope Urban. The bureaucrats did not relent and ordered all men-at-arms to lay down their weapons for inspection.

"Sir Harold informed the bureaucrats that he would lay down his weapons upon the dead bodies of all who stood in his way. The other knights drew their swords and the men-at-arms brought spears and lances to the ready. Will, seeing all of this transpire, had but one thought. 'Commander?' at which the bureaucrats dropped their weapons and began to beg forgiveness from Sir Harold and his party.

'A dreadful mistake,' they cried, and tensions from the continent had all on edge. They bid the travelers welcome from their travels and safe journeys to wherever their destinations may be."

> *Narrator's note: I stopped the tape and asked Amir what caused the local officials who were equally well-armed to relent. He revealed that he placed a vision of them with their heads on spikes, decorating the Tower of London. I resumed recording.*

"'Politicians,' sniffed Sir Harold as he led his party ashore and on to the road to London. The balance of the travelers followed Sir Harold's party, and all looked forward to seeing the great London. London was a city of thirty thousand to fifty thousand inhabitants, much larger and much greater than Paris of the time. Many things had changed since the crusaders left for the Holy Land. William the Conqueror had consolidated his victories at Hastings and inward past London. Slavery was abolished only to be replaced by serfdom to the landed gentry. Those castles that had bowed to William stood, and those that did not had fallen.

"But things were changing. The merchant class and skilled workmen were gaining power. Guilds of carpenters and blacksmiths, iron wrights and shipbuilders, negotiated salaries and work rules as England moved from agrarian to industrial. The Industrial Revolution would not occur for hundreds of years, yet its beginnings were with the end of the Crusades. William's son, Edward II, had given the Wirral family lands and therefor power. This power must be claimed and consolidated, and Will was ready for whatever lay ahead.

"I told Will that I agreed with Sir Harold, and with a single stroke, I could have rendered the bureaucrats into a babbling mob. Will laughed and asked me, "Are they not that already?"

"The old Roman road widened as the party approached London. London was and would continue to be the seat of royalty and power for the island kingdom. Protocol demanded that the returning crusaders call upon the king and swear fealty to him, before returning to their castles and lands. King Edward and Sir Harold were cousins and close allies. Edward II had handed the forfeited lands of another noble to the Wirrals so Will would have no problems swearing loyalty to the Crown.

"It was on the third day of travel from Plymouth that the group entered the city of London and made their way to the castle of King Edward. The roads were not lined with well-wishers or citizens happy at our return, but as we got closer to the king's castle, a group of men-at-arms, squires, and pages cheered our return. Unknown to us, serfs from the fields had been ordered to attend and cheer so it was an altogether glorious experience. King Edward rode out to greet us on a pure white stallion that was of size and strength to pull a castle from its foundation! All in the party bowed and swore fealty to the king as he welcomed us home. To his cousin Harold, he offered additional lands surrounding Nottingham, known as Sherwood Forest, be added to his holdings. Harold was pleased and saluted his cousin with a jeweled broadsword. Edward awarded each knight in turn with additional lands and holdings, naming several to duke and baron titles.

"When Edward recognized William of Wirral, he asked Will to conduct a letter of terms to his uncles by which all might prosper at the families' endeavors. Will bowed deeply and vowed he would conduct the letter to his uncles and that he would be representing his father, Richard, killed in the Crusades to free the Holy Lands and City of Jerusalem. King Edward urged his stallion toward young Will and then ordered him to kneel. Will complied, and the king dismounted, drew his jeweled broadsword, and tapped Will on his right then left shoulder. Edward shouted to all in his presence that this was William, son of Richard of Wirral, and that he had found favor in the sight of his king and his subjects.

"Word had traveled of mighty deeds and loyal service to his king and to his God. And with the words 'Rise, Sir William of Wirral.'

The family would obtain a peerage and all that it encompassed. Edward then presented Will with an exquisite broadsword, heavily jeweled and bearing silver and gold inlays. 'Take this as evidence of our presentation here today.' Will was fairly sure that this was the sword of the former nobleman who lost his lands, holdings, and head at the hands of King Edward. No matter. Will felt he was on the right side of history today. This would add credibility to his claim to his father's holdings and strengthen his position with his uncles and their families. Tomorrow, he would travel to his homeland alone. Of course I would be with him. It would take two days to cover the distance and give Sir William time to formulate his plan.

"Sir Harold and the other knights encircled Sir William and congratulated him by beating swords and lances on their shields. The men-at-arms saluted Will as they dropped to one knee and presented their spears forward. Will was overwhelmed at the prospect of being a tradesman/knight and what his family crest would include. I was amused at the pomp and ritual and deemed it all worthless in the greater scheme of things. Will, however, knew what a peerage entailed and the power it could bring to his family so he did not discount the presentation.

Eighteen

The Contract
London, early fall 1101

"After the presentation, King Edward asked Sir Harold and the newly knighted Sir William to join him for a private dinner and discussion. Great sides of beef and wild pheasants were served along with barley cakes, black bread, grapes, and apples. Large flagons of beer and wine were presented along with cups of mead and spirituous whiskeys. It was a grand feast, the like Will had never seen. After all had eaten and drunk their fill, the king drew Harold and Will near to his seat and offered another round of congratulations.

"To Will, the king explained his reasoning behind the knighthood. All of the praises Edward had professed at the ceremony were true but not the entire story. He had given the confiscated castle and lands to the Wirral family for their loyalty and devotion to the Crown and to their countrymen. All of the brothers were savvy businessmen along with being skilled tradesmen. It was the king's hope to open the ports around the peninsula to increase trade with Ireland, western Scotland, and the Nordic states to the north and east. Additionally, having a thriving port on the Irish Sea would prevent nations, such as Spain and the Netherlands, from blockading needed materials during times of war. Edward had full confidence in the brothers and Sir William. However, castles and landholdings were the realm of nobles and peers. He needed to knight at least one brother to mollify other nobles, lest they think we are tearing the fabric of society asunder. Who better to knight than a storied young hero just back from a successful crusade to the Holy Lands?

"Edward continued that this would set the precedent for him to name each brother as a *baron* within a year's time. King Edward handed Will a document closed with the royal seal so all would know its authenticity. He explained that within the documents were permits and deeds allowing the Wirral family to establish trading posts, money changing houses, farm markets, warehouses, and other businesses necessary to allow the region to flourish. Taxes to the Crown would be set at 10 percent yearly with no other tribute collected. The family was free to set prices, establish local governmental offices, collect local taxes, and establish a local constabulary (including sheriff) to assure the peace and arrest the lawless. The documents also explained the need for a knighthood and why he had chosen Will. Sir Harold chimed in that this was a great honor for the Wirral family and that he shared the king's expectations of what the future held.

"Will agreed with all the items in the document and assured the king that his uncles would understand and agree also. At this, the king ushered Sir Harold and Sir William outside to his stables and waved at an attending squire. The squire bowed and went inside the corral, returning with the most beautiful horse Will had ever seen. It was a two-year-old male colt. It was also obvious that the colt would not grow into a huge draft or war animal. Its lines were sleek, highly muscled, but not heavy. Its legs seemed way out of portion to the rest of its body. It was the color of dark honey with a large white patch on its face. The mane was a deep, rich brown and shone in contrast to the dark honey body.

"The king spoke up that the colt had been a gift to him from a returning crusader who said it was of pure, Arabian stock. The king continued that he really had no use for such an animal and suggested Will keep it as a pet. Will readily accepted the gift and moved to touch the colt and reassure him. The colt allowed Will's touch and eagerly brushed its head against Will's back when he turned to face the king and Sir Harold. Again Will expressed his thanks to the king for such a wonderful gift. The king nodded to the squire who was standing to one side, and the squire took the colt's lead and drew him back into the corral enclosure.

"The king and his knights said their good evenings, and Harold and Will departed toward the camp. As they walked, Sir Harold asked Will if he was concerned about his uncles' reaction to his knighthood. Will told Sir Harold that he had not seen his uncles or anyone else in his family in over six years but what he remembered were strong family bonds and delight in the accomplishments of any family member. He supposed there may be some initial jealousy, but he felt sure as the king's documents were explained to them that they would understand and rejoice in their entire good fortune. Sir Harold pressed Will and asked if he would allow several men-at-arms to accompany Will to his homelands and family so that he would not face them alone. Will's reply was that he would not be alone.

"When Will was back in his tent and without company, he conveyed the thought 'Commander, did you hear and understand?' I, who had the mind link open during the entire conversation with the king, answered with a single thought. 'Yes.' I searched Will's memories and found no fear of his uncles. In fact, I found a very strong bond of love and respect. I questioned Will as to why the king and Sir Harold seemed so worried about a negative reaction from his uncles to Will's knighthood. Will replied that wealth and power, greed and avarice had broken many families in the past but that he would not let that happen to the Wirrals. I continued that I would be with him when he met the uncles and (in a slightly ominous tone) would tolerate no moves against him. Sir William smiled and said out loud to me, 'That is why I told Sir Harold I would not be alone.'"

Nineteen

The Chance Encounter
Wirral Peninsula, early fall 1101

"It took Will three days to travel to his home near the River Mersey and just south of the Irish Sea. He packed his belongings and his father's remaining tools into a wagon pulled by two very large oxen. Will tied the Arabian to the back of the wagon, and it followed along without protest. Will had walked to Damascus and back so he saw no reason not to walk the last few miles home. In spite of Sir Harold's protestations, Will traveled alone—or as alone as he could be with the small box and very large jinn inside. He followed well-established roads dating back to the times of the Romans and found himself at peace in the heavily forested lands leading to the peninsula. The leaves of the huge trees were turning brilliant red and yellow as the air virtually snapped with the crispness of autumn.

"As he passed small farms and villages, all were busy with the fall harvest and preservation of winter stores. Squirrels and hedgehogs scurried about gathering their own provisions for the coming season, and migratory birds were moving inland and south. Will loved this time of year as his father would have been busy repairing farm implements and wagon wheels. Will would have been at his side, smiling and wondering if he would ever be so strong and wise as his father.

"There were several times like this when Will's thoughts had returned to his father and the great loss that he bore alone. Many times before, Will sought a quiet place to be alone and ended up crying scalding tears of loss. In the end, however, his sense of duty and purpose imbued into him by his father, Father Joseph, Benazir, King Edward, Sir Harold, and even me would rescue him. His destiny lay in Wirral, and his purpose was his duty to others. He could read and write many languages. He used the mathematics and architectural skills of the classical philosophers and scientists, and he possessed the knowledge and skill in the healing arts that were far superior to anyone on the island of Britain. His purpose was to bring these gifts of knowledge and skill to his family and the people of his homeland. Will was happy with this destiny and also satisfied.

"On the third day's travel, the road passed an abandoned manor house with barns and out-buildings surrounding a large, open expanse. There were riding stables and empty barracks scattered about and at least two natural springs near the manor house, each with its own well house. Just to the south of the manor house at the edge of the expanse stood a single English oak. Will looked in amazement at its ninety-foot height and its crown spread of at least one hundred feet. It would have taken ten large men, arm to arm, to have encircled its trunk at the base.

"The tree was known as the French oak on the continent, and barrels made from its wood were excellent for aging the wines of Burgundy and Champagne. This one, however, was enormous! Will turned the oxen toward the tree and had only proceeded a few yards when he heard a female voice of Nordic origin call out, demanding to know who he was and what business he had there.

"Will could not see where the voice was originating but answered that he was Sir William of Wirral, returning this day from almost six years in the Crusades of the Holy Land. At once, a young woman of no more than sixteen years stepped out from behind the huge oak.

She was dressed in peasant garb but was armed with an English longbow and quiver of arrows. She was tall, standing almost six feet, with the long, blonde hair and the fierce blue eyes of a Viking.

"As she stepped out from behind the tree, she pulled an arrow from the quiver and placed it on the bow. She did not draw back but eyed Will and his oxcart closely. Then her gaze turned to the Arabian behind the cart and an almost involuntary gasp escaped her throat. With no threat left in her voice, she said to Will that this was the most beautiful horse she had ever seen. Will asked her if she had ever seen an Arabian like this one, to which she said she had not. Will pressed her with several more questions. Who was she? Why was she on this abandoned land? What was her name?

"Without taking her eyes off the Arabian, she told Will that she, along with her mother, was in service to the noble of the manor. Several months before, soldiers came and took the noble and his family away. They had no place to go so stayed here and cared for the livestock the soldiers did not take. Her mother recently found out that a new group of people in Wirral would be taking over the manor and grounds and left to meet with them and ask to continue at the manor in service to the new owners. The girl remembered that Will had introduced himself to her as Sir William of Wirral and asked if he knew the new owners. Will laughed and told her that he and his family were the new owners and that he was on his way home to see his family for the first time in six years.

"The girl snipped that Will did not appear to be a knight or nobleman, walking in front of an oxcart. Will laughed again and told her that seventy-two hours ago, he was an apprentice blacksmith. The girl looked bewildered so Will reached into the oxcart and showed her the tools of his trade. She was even more skeptical and challenged Will to prove his claim of nobility, at which Sir William drew the jeweled broadsword of a knight and noble. Her stance softened a bit, but Will could see this was all too much for her to understand at one time. Again Will asked her name, and she whispered, 'Kyrie.'

"Will bowed deeply to the girl and told her it was a pleasure to meet 'Valkyrie, Chooser of the Slain.' Kyrie was completely taken aback by Will's knowledge of her name and its meaning. She asked him how he came to know these things, and Will told Kyrie of his mother's ancestry and his fondness for languages. Will proposed that Kyrie accompany him to Wirral and meet his family. Perhaps they would find her mother there as well. She could walk beside the Arabian and become acquainted to the horse and to Will as he further explained his travels and the events leading up to today. Kyrie removed the arrow from the longbow and placed it back in the quiver. She then slung the longbow over her shoulder. For the first time since seeing Will, she smiled at him. For the first time since seeing Kyrie, he realized she was beautiful."

Twenty

Love and Friendship
Wirral Peninsula, fall 1101

"I had been following the conversation between Will and Kyrie but did not intervene or try to establish the mind link. I found this entire biological dance to be strange at best and unfathomable at least. My first impressions of Kyrie were favorable as one would find a certain tapestry more favorable than another. She did have courage and did not look to be one who would surrender any ground in a fight. I also gave a passing glance at the enormous English oak that Will had marveled over. I agreed it was big! But mostly, I was content (not very often) at how the trip had transpired. My human host was a boy—er, man of good character and constantly sought opportunities to expand his earthly wisdom. He was brave and exceedingly wise for one his age. He had been knighted by the current, earthly king of the region, and he had not completely destroyed any chance of producing offspring by disinterest or dishonesty with a potential mate. After all, for a human, he was getting along in years! I decided I would talk to Will tonight, privately!

"Will built a large fire that effectively beat back the chill of autumn and spread his bedding across the soft turf of the pastureland they had chosen for the night's camp. Tomorrow, they would be at

Will's home and his kinsmen's reaction to his knighthood would be revealed. Kyrie hoped to find her mother but feared she may find herself alone in a foreign land. The oxen were settled in and the Arabian was gleefully happy to be close to Kyrie. The colt had obviously imprinted on her and would follow her wherever she went. Kyrie was no less engaged with the colt as she led her around the camp and taught her to take food from her hand.

"As the fire crackled and spit sparks toward the heavens, Will told Kyrie of his travels to the Holy Lands, his works with Father Joseph at the abbey, and his father's untimely death as they returned to Britain at the will of the new King Edward. Kyrie listened intently but asked few questions. When Will finished his saga, Kyrie studied his eyes carefully. She took several minutes to offer any response at all, but when she did, it was startling to Will. Kyrie said that she understood and believed Will's story but had the feeling that he had left out some strange, external force or entity that weaved its way throughout the tale. Will admitted that some protective angel must have intervened on occasion, and that appeared to satisfy the girl. Will's brain resonated with my strongest baritone voice as I sniffed loudly, 'Angel indeed!'

"As Will related his story, Kyrie settled upon the bedding Will provided and was prone, leaning on one shoulder as she listened. Will saw her high cheekbones framed with her blonde hair, her large and fierce blue eyes, and full lips in the flickering firelight, and the more he saw, the more he wanted to see. Kyrie was also observant of Will's broad shoulders, large and powerful arms, fierce blue eyes, yet gentle demeanor. An attraction had been struck, but shyness ruled the night.

"When all discussion had ended and sleep was upon them, I opened the mind link with Will and said, 'I am with your thoughts.' Will grumbled and thought to Amir that he had not requested the mind link, to which I replied that Will's request was not requested either. Knowing that I was resolute, Will's thoughts projected, 'Commander!' to which I dutifully replied, 'I am with your thoughts.'

"I projected that I approved of this female. She appeared to be intelligent, brave, and without any visible physical deformity. My opinion was that she and Will complete any premarriage rituals necessary and get married (since that seemed to be the custom) without delay. I also suggested that they endeavor to produce as many offspring as reasonable in the shortest amount of time allowable. Will's mind chuckled as he told me that he was, indeed, struck by this girl but that such things needed to proceed slowly so as not to alarm the other party. My harrumph to Will's brain was almost audible! Besides, one quick trip into her subconscious revealed a strong attraction to Will. The courtship dance would remain an enigma to me. I did, however, give both Will and Kyrie pleasant dreams and a full night's sleep. My thoughts turned to the pragmatic as I wished that Will and Kyrie remain together, in matrimony, and both work with him to find the key to my freedom—a noble cause indeed!

"With the morning sunrise, Will arose and shook off the evening's chill and layer of fresh dew that was sticking to his garments. He strode over to the dwindling fire and replenished its core with dry sticks and other kindling. Soon the fire roared again, and its warmth soothed Will against the autumn chill. Kyrie was still sleeping soundly, and it was only when the Arabian nudged her with her head that she stirred. Kyrie yawned and stretched her arms outward and upward. Her eyelids fluttered and opened, revealing the fierce blue eyes of a warrior-princess. Her eyes met Will's gaze, and she blushed slightly as she smiled and wished him a good morning. Will had not taken his eyes away from her. It seemed impossible to look elsewhere. In all of his travels, not once had he encountered a creature as beautiful as Kyrie. She shattered his daydream with the words 'Do you not wish me a good morning too?'

"Will instantly was embarrassed and failed miserably at several attempts of apologies. He finally was able to put together the words for a morning's greeting and invited her closer to the fire. Now fully recovered from his most recent social failings, Will told Kyrie that they would be at the family homestead by midday. He also hoped that her mother would be there to greet her. Will would make the introductions of Kyrie and her mother to all of his family. He would propose that Kyrie and her mother stay in the employ of the Wirral family as they planned the future of themselves as individuals and the future of the newly acquired lands and manor. Kyrie said that she would like that and it would be wonderful to stay near the Arabian as it grew into adulthood.

"Will broke out the last of the provisions—mostly bread and several cheeses along with some local fruit and nuts he had found. The day was full of promise as the sun rose in a steel-blue sky. The air was already warming and dispelling the evening chill. Will put out the fire and hitched the two oxen to the cart. Kyrie took the Arabian's lead and a position beside Will as they set off toward their destiny. Will's mind was full of possibilities and wonderful potential. But what of Amir? He had promised to help his friend (the first time he had ever referred to me in that manner), and he meant to keep that promise. I, of course, was eavesdropping on all of the conversations but was taken aback by Will's reference to me as 'friend.' In all of his history, no entity had ever referred to me as 'friend.'"

Narrator's note: When the recording session was over, I informed Amir that I would be unable to meet with him the following day due to several physician appointments, an MRI, and a PET scan. He seemed slightly put off but agreed to reschedule our next session in forty-eight hours. Then he did something that he had never done: question the necessity of my cancer treatments. I was immediately concerned and somewhat frightened.

Twenty One

Kyrie's Tale
Wirral Peninsula, fall 1101

"The sun was rising quickly as Will and Kyrie traveled the ancient Roman road toward the Wirral Peninsula and Will's family's homesteads. As they walked, Will asked Kyrie how it was that she came to this part of the world. He recognized that she was not Anglo-Saxon by heritage but Norse due to her name and traits. Kyrie told Will that she had been born in a village to the north that had been established by Vikings several hundred years before. It was not uncommon that Viking raiders and then traders would establish a colony on the islands. Her father had died of his injuries in a raid by an unknown tribe of warriors. He had fought well and ultimately, with local defenders, saved the village from being overrun and plundered. But he suffered mortal wounds during the battle and died two days later. Kyrie continued that she and her mother wrapped his wounds and cared for him as best they could but could not save him. It was his last wish that Kyrie and her mother travel south to find more peaceable lands and inhabitants.

"Kyrie told Will how they traveled alone and under the cover of night so as not to attract unwanted attention. All of their possessions were packed in sacks, carried on their backs, including their meager rations. After several days of travel, they had come upon a farmhouse and approached the residents for help. As luck would have it, the farmer, wife, and five children were devout Christians and asked mother and daughter to stay with them a while to rest and provision.

"Then Kyrie smiled as she finished her story. She told Will that her mother thanked the family profusely but asked why they would share their home and food with travelers they did not know. The farmer smiled at them and then his family as he said, 'Do ye not know the parable of the Samaritan?' Kyrie told Will that she and her mother stayed with the family for two days and accepted some preserved foods suitable for traveling. The last gift from the farmer was to set our course to the manor house. He said that a great nobleman lived there and that he had heard of people joining his staff working in and around the manor and stables.

Kyrie and her mother walked for three more days before finding the manor and its owner. They were immediately hired and put to work by an overseer—Kyrie's mother in the kitchen and Kyrie in the stables. Kyrie told Will that her work was hard and smelly but she did so love the animals. The other stable workers were young boys who did not have any family. They teased her at first, but when she won the first fight with the biggest stable boy, they relented and accepted her. One of the stable boys had an English longbow but absolutely could not use it. Kyrie had been taught the bow by her father for years and was quite proficient. She would give lessons to the stable boys who were interested, and they would bring her fruit and sweets that were to be tossed out by the nobleman.

"All seemed to be working out for several weeks until early one morning, soldiers from London came and took the nobleman away. Most of the staff ran away, fearing that they might be arrested or even killed. Kyrie said that she and her mother hid out behind the stables as several soldiers came and took most of the horses and oxen away. However, they did not take all, and she and her mother decided to stay and care for the manor and the animals until such time that the new owners arrived or the nobleman was restored.

Either way, they believed they would be rewarded for tending the estate and not letting it deteriorate.

"There was plenty of food for both the humans and the animals to last the winter, which would soon be approaching. Kyrie's mother heard days later from a passing traveler that the new owners were to be found at a village in Wirral. She asked directions and was told to follow the old Roman road north for one half day's travel and she would find the Wirrals. Kyrie's mother left only yesterday when Will had appeared.

"Will thanked her for her story and praised both her mother's and her bravery and resourcefulness. Will asked Kyrie what her mother's and father's names were. Kyrie replied that her mother was called Blinda and her father was Erik. Will told Kyrie that he would say two prayers tonight: one that Blinda had found her way to his village and one to give thanks that Erik had sent them here to him. The blush on Kyrie's cheeks was prominent as she looked up and asked Will if that was his village. Will turned forward to see the River Mersey on his right and the village of Wirral on his left. After six years and all that had transpired, he was home! Will turned back to Kyrie with a look of relief and accomplishment and said, 'Yes. This is home!'"

The Homecoming
Wirral homesteads, fall 1101

"From where Will and Kyrie stood, the heavily wooded forest opened up into a pleasant meadow of small grasses and shrubs enveloping the village. In the center of the village was a wellhouse that provided fresh water to the entire village from an artesian spring. The water literally poured upward into the well then divided into northwestern and southwestern branches flowing toward the River Mersey. Surrounding the central well house were six neatly situated homesteads: one for each uncle and aunt in the family. The closest dwelling was the home of Will's aunt Laura. She had been widowed several years before Will and his father had departed for the Crusades.

"Laura was in charge of the entire village's food storage and preservation for sale to nearby villages and for survival of her clan and farm animals in the winter. She was expert in the dry storage of harvested grains, such as wheat, rye, barley, and oats. She was also skilled at drying freshly butchered meats from the cattle, sheep, and pigs that were raised by her sister and Will's aunt Ann. A small group of subterranean caverns to the north of the village, where the temperature remained that of a winter's morning, provided safe storage for some perishables like potatoes, onions, and cabbages along with fresh milk, cheeses, butters, and fruit compotes.

"To the right of Laura's home lived Will's aunt Ann and her husband, Thomas. Together with their four boys, they managed all of the livestock and pasturelands belonging to the family. Among the farm animals were four oxen, two draft horses, a herd of about fifty sheep, and several sows with multiple piglets. In addition to animal husbandry, Ann's family harvested animals for food and sale and had become quite talented butchers. They worked closely with Laura in the preservation and preparation of meat from the stock. The family presided over the annual sheepshearing, providing raw wool for sale to the fabric makers in Flanders. Ann and Thomas also managed the barns, stables, and stockades to the north and west of the central well house.

"To the west of Laura's home lived Donald, his wife, Mary, and their two girls. Donald was the village carpenter and was responsible for all of the wood structures in the building of homes, shops, barns, and stables. Donald fancied himself an artist with his favorite medium being wood from the surrounding forests. His repertoire included furniture, beds for babies, splints for broken bones, and coffins for laying the dead to rest. Mary was a sturdy woman and relished working with her husband in their shop, just behind the three barns they had constructed years ago. The girls, like their mother, were strong and not afraid to carry logs for making boards or loading newly built furniture into an oxcart for market.

"Farther north was the home of Will's father, Richard—now his home. It had been carefully cared for and maintained during the years of the Crusades. Normally, Will would have followed in his father's footsteps and taken over the blacksmith craft as part of the entire family's enterprise. But this was not going to be a normal succession from father to son. The documents that Will carried would change all of their lives forever.

"Two of the other three homes belonged to Andrew, wife Sarah, and three children, and Emma, husband, and one boy of Will's age. Both families were farmers, each farming about fifty acres of mostly wheat but including some rye, barley, and oats. They were efficient farmers and typically grew enough grains not only to ensure subsistence but also to sell at the marketplace or nearby villages.

"The last home belonged to Will's uncle Charles. Next to Richard, Charles was the oldest and largest brother; he was barrel-chested with huge arms. Charles was a woodsman. His craft was to provide wood for building, fuel, and sale. The woods surrounding the Wirral homesteads were dense and populated with ample hardwoods, fragrant conifers, flowering understory trees, wild grape vines, and several fruit trees. This was harvesttime and Charles was busy gathering ripening grapes and fruit from apple and wild cherry trees. Wild tree nuts were abundant along with bushels of acorns that rendered a fine cooking oil. The forest was also populated by rabbits, pheasants, and doves that provided extra meat and diversity to the table. Lastly, Charles was expert at finding and extracting wild honey from hives hidden among dead and fallen trees. Charles's wife, Marion, had died tragically seventeen years ago while giving birth to their first child. He never remarried. Will loved and respected all of his aunts and uncles, but he held a special bond with Charles.

"Will and Kyrie moved down a slight hill and toward the homesteads. As they neared the homesteads, Will threw back his head and yelled, 'Hello!' to the village. Within a few seconds, people emerged from the shops and cottages to see who had called them. It was Charles, just coming back from gathering grapes, recognized Will. He stood motionless for a mere second before tossing the grapes aside and running at full speed to greet his nephew. Charles never slowed as he tackled Will and the two went sprawling across the meadow, laughing hysterically.

"Unknown to Will, Charles, or me, a small crack appeared in the box that imprisoned me. Charles and Will rose to their knees and embraced each other in a vicelike hug, close to breaking a rib. Kyrie and the Arabian were naturally startled at the mock attack but quickly realized the joy of this homecoming. By the time Will and

Charles had regained their feet, all of the village had raced to Will, each trying to embrace him, kiss him, but most of all welcome him home. Will wished he could extend this moment of family and joy forever.

"With all of the merriment of Will's homecoming, Kyrie noticed a single, female figure shading her eyes to see what was going on. Kyrie immediately recognized her mother and broke into a full run, dragging the Arabian behind her. As Kyrie called out to her mother, Blinda recognized the figure running toward her and also ran to embrace her daughter. It was Charles who pointed toward the mother and daughter as they greeted each other. 'Another homecoming?' To which Will replied, 'I hope so!'"

Twenty Three

Discussions of Future and Past
Wirral Peninsula, fall 1101

"Over the next few days, there was merriment and feasting at Will's homecoming. There was also sadness as Will told of men that were lost to the Saracens and this father's death at the hands of bandits. He told of his emptiness in killing the child who put the crossbow bolt into his father's chest. But he also told the family of his education in the ancient arts and sciences and his mastery of languages and translations of ancient scrolls. He did not tell them about me.

"'Are you ashamed of me?' I questioned sarcastically in Will's mind. Will simply rolled his eyes! Each aunt and uncle also had stories to tell of crops and drought, children being born, and new marketplaces being formed. They were witnessing the beginnings of a significant change in the economics of the land. Blinda and Kyrie were invited to be a part of the discussions since they had firsthand knowledge of the manor house and lands surrounding it. I actually insisted that they be present. Will had presented the documents from King Edward explaining his knighthood, the king's wishes, and the rewards that would come from making those wishes into reality. Will wisely asked all to return home and consider what actions they as individuals and a family should take in order to understand the possibilities. Charles, who was now the family patriarch, agreed, and the uncles, aunts, husbands, wives, and multiple children returned to their individual cottages, except Blinda and Kyrie. Will offered his home to them for as long as they were in Wirral. He would ask his uncle Charles for a corner to occupy, or he could pitch his tent as he had done for the last six years.

"Will and Charles accompanied Blinda and Kyrie to his cottage. His family had been diligent in keeping it ready for his and his father's return. Laura was moments behind them with fresh bread, dried meats, wild grapes, and fresh milk for their dinner. The water basins were filled, and the fireplace soon was roaring with seasoned hardwoods. The cottage now smelled of new life and simple foods. Will, Charles, and Laura bid the mother and daughter good night and departed toward Charles's cottage. Once alone, Blinda and Kyrie embraced again and then said prayers for their food and good fortune in finding this family. As they ate their supper, they talked about how they could assist the family in their new ventures. Blinda remarked that luck and the king had smiled on the Wirrals and that she and Kyrie could do much worse in another noble's house.

"Blinda smiled at Kyrie in a sly fashion and asked what she thought of the young, educated blacksmith who was now knight and nobleman. The fierceness in Kyrie's blue eyes softened into a dreamy stare out into an unknown place. Kyrie replied that young Sir William was kind and generous to her from the first time they had met. She continued that newly knighted or not, he was chivalrous and a gentleman at all times and it was he who had asked her to travel together to find her. Blinda's slyness did not retreat as she remarked to Kyrie that Sir William was also incredibly handsome, or had she not noticed? Kyrie had noticed! After supper, as they prepared for the night, Blinda offered one last comment that she also thought Sir William's uncle Charles seemed nice!

"Charles, Laura, and Will sat down at round table that Donald had built years ago. I requested the mind link of Will to fully understand the topics to be discussed. I also promised not to interrupt. The mortals discussed the information that had been revealed in the king's document and that fortune had surely smiled upon the entire family. Will told them that he was formulating a pathway that he would like to present as a basis for moving forward with the king's plans. The plan could be amended and altered so as to include all family members and that all should be in agreement before implementing any plan.

"Laura and Charles agreed with Will's idea and asked him when he thought it would be ready to present to the family. Will replied that he would be ready in three days. Laura arose to leave for her cottage then turned to Will and asked if Kyrie might be in these plans. Will smiled and said he would ask if she would like to be included. Charles stood up to escort Laura out the door and asked that Will also included the girl's mother. Will and Laura looked at each other in amazement before Will agreed to talk to Blinda as well. With that, Charles announced that he needed a walk to clear his mind before sleep. Laura then said to Will that she did not think a walk would clear Charles's thoughts of this new, mature, yet beautiful woman."

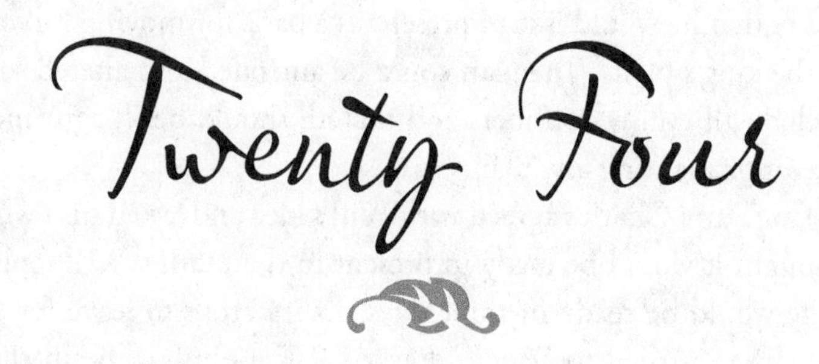

Economics for the Future
Wirral Homesteads, fall 1101

"Three days passed and the Wirral extended family met in one of the barns. Again, I requested the mind link to understand the proceedings. Tables and chairs had been brought in for the meeting along with food, water, and several jars of wine made from the wild grapes in Charles's forest. Will was the last to arrive, accompanied by Blinda and Kyrie (and me). As all were settled, Charles rose to speak. He proposed to open the meeting with a prayer of thanksgiving to God and the Christ from whom all blessings flow (to quote the 'Old Hundredth' Psalm). The group repeated the psalm in prayer, and when all had said their amens, Charles proposed a round of wine for all.

"Laughter erupted, but Charles protested that he was in earnest and to serve the wine to all attending. Most in the family (except Will's father, Richard), knew better than to argue too long with Charles, and cups of the red beverage were served to all. Charles surveyed the family to ensure that all had a cup of wine, and then he spoke again. Charles proposed a toast of thanksgiving for the return of young Will, now Sir William, and a second toast in remembrance of their departed kinsman, Richard. Cups and cheers were raised for Will as all drank to his return and good health. Charles raised his cup a second time while saying only the words 'To our brother Richard.' Everyone repeated Richard's name and drank.

"Will rose to speak, thanking his family for their toasts of thanksgiving and remembrance. Today, he would present a plan that would affect the future of every Wirral and potentially other families for the next century! His proposal was that every head of household in the Wirral clan would form a holding company. Every spouse and child of the holding company members would become heirs, and the number of members could grow as new kinsmen came of age to lead a division of thc holding company—unless a cap number of members was agreed upon. The divisions would be forestry headed by Charles; wheat production led by Andrew and his family; rye, barley, and oat production led by Emma and her family; all woodcraft and building materials headed by Donald and his family; and all food storage activities headed by his aunt Laura.

"Donald rose to question who would manage the manor house and the surrounding lands and forests and what would happen to his father's blacksmith trade. Will asked who had been operating the blacksmith shop in his and his father's absence. Charles answered that several people had run the trade but that a younger man from the village of Chester and his wife had done the best job and were hoping to hire on if the need was there. Will replied that he would like to meet this man and his wife. Will asked their names, to which Charles replied, 'Mathew and Kaitlyn.'

"As for the manor house, Will proposed it be converted into an inn for travelers. The manor house was situated on the intersection of both north-south and east-west Roman roads. The north-south road went from Cornwall and Devon in the south to Liverpool, Nottingham, and on to Edinburgh in Scotland. The east-west traveled the length of the Wirral Peninsula to Norfolk, Suffolk, and branches to London and Dover. This was sure to be a busy intersection with travelers needing lodging, food, drink, livery, blacksmithing, and other items.

"Will said that he would move to the manor house to manage and build the stables and horse-breeding operations while hiring Blinda and Kyrie to manage the inn. The family council nodded in approval, but then Emma rose to question where the wealth and currency were to afford such a large enterprise until it could become profitable and self-sustaining. 'How is it that we can hire workers and overseers, such as Blinda and Kyrie, for the manor house and young Mathew and his wife for the blacksmith shop?' Will reached into his belt and retrieved the bag given him by Sir Robert of Normandy when he had healed his Arabian foal in Calais. Will emptied the contents of the bag onto a table to the audible gasp of the group. As multiple pounds of gold, Roman, Saracen, and Greek coins of multiple denominations bounced and rolled about, Will said that he had concluded that there was enough gold on the table to build the infrastructure of his proposed group of businesses, hire the workers and overseers, and sustain the entire family for two years if necessary. The barn went completely silent!

"Charles rose to speak and asked the six family members if they would join in the enterprise and promise to support it for at least two years before another question would be raised to continue or not. Laura rose and faced Will then asked the question all wanted to ask. She asked Will what he wanted in order to almost single-handedly fund this major project. Will's response was short. He wished to be the single contact with King Edward so that the king's wishes and rewards were aligned, he wished to be allowed to teach the children of Wirral the classic knowledge of the ancients, and he wished the continued love and support he had felt since his return from the Crusades.

"Will sat down as Charles asked the question again. This time, Ann rose along with her husband and daughter. Ann said that she was in favor of the idea but that she had questions about the equal distribution of profits. What if an entire barley crop were to fail? How could her family survive without the support of other family members?

"I popped a thought into Will's mind. 'She won't lose a crop. I do have some power over the weather!'

"Will arose again to address Ann and her family. He said that at harvesttime, all of the crops necessary to sustain the family would be stored. But there was always about 20 percent extra that usually was sold and would be again to form the profit that would be turned over to the holding company. All family units would do the same, regardless of the profit percentage. When all profits were within the holding company, 10 percent would be sent to King Edward along with their accounting. Of the remaining 90 percent, most would be divided and shared among the six heads of households. They would decide on a percentage to withhold in case of emergencies or new opportunities that arose.

"Will emphasized that the family would support each other in good times and bad as they had always done. Will said that he would be the keeper of the accounting and that the family would meet regularly to discuss the current finances. Again, heads nodded in approval, and again, Charles rose to speak. He thanked Will for the proposal and the answers he offered to the questions of his kinsmen.

"Charles posed the question a third time, and all arose in the barn and shouted, 'Yes!'

"Will glanced over to Laura, then Donald, Andrew, Emma, Ann, Blinda, and finally Kyrie, before saying, 'Then let us begin!'

"This was when I sensed something was wrong with my prison of so many years. I could feel a change but did not know what had happened. I did know that a sense of dread was building up within me. This was unlike any sensation I had ever experienced, and I did not like it!"

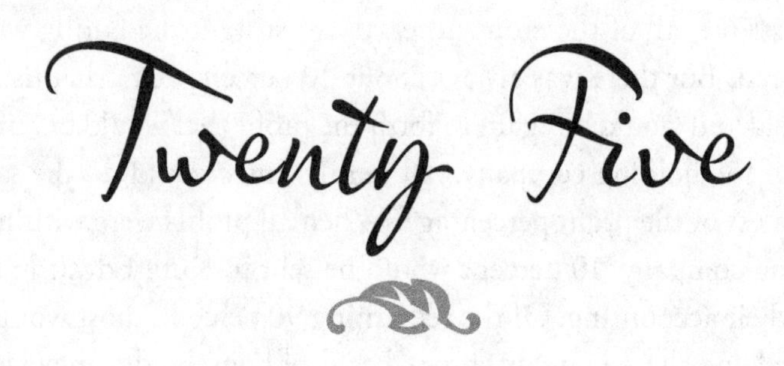

Twenty Five

Let Us Begin
Wirral Peninsula, winter 1101

"With winter upon them, the family focused on preparing the manor house and its grounds to become an inn, stables, and shops. Donald and his family along with Charles began work on the manor house to turn it into an inn. Rooms were subdivided into bedrooms, of which twenty-three rooms became available. Blinda and Kyrie laid out the kitchen and dining rooms along with a library, lobby, and spectacular ballroom. Will met Mathew and Kaitlyn, hiring them instantly to take on the blacksmith trade at the homesteads and also at the manor house stables. Emma and Andrew and their families prepared the grounds around the manor house to accept seed for the spring plantings of fresh vegetables. Charles hired ten men from the village of Chester to assist him in providing trees and logs to the manor house projects and Donald's expert hands. Laura experimented with earthen vessels to transport fresh and preserved foods to the manor house. Will brought healing powers to all who needed them, and the entire family experienced a robust and misery-free winter.

"As spring approached, focus was turned toward the large wheat fields and barley, rye, and oat fields around Wirral to be planted.

The spring was unusually mild with moderate temperatures and necessary rain. The manor house was nearing completion of its renovations, and the barns and stables were completely refurbished and ready for livestock. Mathew and Kaitlyn had established the blacksmith trade both on Wirral and at the manor house. Will had approached King Edward, and he was pleased with the progress of the new enterprises. Edward was so pleased that he rewarded Will and the family another bag of coins from the Crusades.

"Will hired young men to travel the Roman roads—north and south and east and west—proclaiming the new inn and shops that were available to all travelers. As the Roman roads swelled with travelers, so did the guests at the new inn: pilgrims on their way to Canterbury, knights and nobles with entourages on their way to London, and merchants and warehousemen seeking goods to trade and store. All began to unfold as Will had foreseen. I assisted, providing favorable weather and excellent growing conditions along with giving the minds of travelers a gentle 'push' toward the inn.

"However, I could not escape the increasing sense of impending doom. All seemed to be working well with the mortals, and I could not pinpoint the source of this angst. Several times I wished to broach the subject with Will but felt it would signify weakness. This I could not do! Will also sensed a change in my demeanor and personality. He attempted to engage me on this topic several times but was quickly and utterly dismissed on every occasion.

"But then again, all was going well with the plans. As a harbinger of good fortune, King Edward visited the manor house, bringing with him twenty Arabian colts, both male and female, obtained from the Crusades. It was the king's wish that Will and his family use this stock to breed a race of horses that were strong, reliable, durable, and above all, very fast to provide to his knights and men-at-arms. Will was without words to express his joy and thankfulness to the king. Of course he would take on this task for his king and benefactor.

"One early spring evening on the grounds of the manor house, when Will was alone, he called out to me, 'Commander,' to which I answered, 'I am with your thoughts.' Will began that he was concerned with my temperament and was at once interrupted by a loud and forceful thought from me that echoed throughout his brain. I asked with a heavy measure of sarcasm what concern Will could have regarding 'the commander.' Will continued that I had not seemed as engaged with the work and progress going on all around them. Will also offered that my assistance had been invaluable toward the success of all of the enterprises and that neither he nor his family could ever hope to repay me. Will said that in all of my assistance to him and his family, the single missing element was the joy he used to experience when he engaged with the family. Will ended his thoughts with an appeal to me: to let him help in any way to regain that lost joy.

"I was silent for several minutes, but although I was not transmitting thoughts, I was still actively linked to Will's mind. Will fought the impulse to reach out again to me and waited for a response. After several more agonizing seconds, I began to transmit my thoughts. I admitted to Will that he had been troubled since arriving at the Wirral homesteads. I did not approach Will with this sense of trouble because I could not identify its source. In recent days, I identified that the change was related to my box/prison. I continued that I never felt fear for anything in heaven or on earth, save a respect for the Most High. Will interrupted me this time with the thought that he could think of many words to describe me, but fearful or afraid would not be on that list. My mood lightened slightly at the offhand compliment. I continued that my main concerns with existence as an immortal were to be free again, reconciled to the Most High, and to not be swept away into the parallel existence, awaiting judgment and having no interaction with anyone or anything. To me, this existence would be like death.

"As Will listened to the painful thoughts of his friend and companion, he tried to remember any events that may have triggered the deep and troubling feelings that I had begun to experience.

Almost instantly, a flash of a memory appeared in Will's mind. I saw it too. The memory was of Charles running to greet him on the first day back home. He remembered the tackle at full speed and both men hitting the ground hard, rolling about in their joyous greeting. Will desperately reached into the leather pouch attached to his waist belt to produce the small box of Palestine oak and vessel containing me. Will brought the box close to his eye to inspect its integrity. His next thoughts to me were shouts of 'Oh my God! Oh my God!'"

Twenty Six

Imminent Disaster

The Manor House Grounds, early spring 1102

"Will's hands shook and his mind spun as he surveyed the oak box. There was a small crack in the side of the box and an obvious flaw in the seal of the lid of the box. These breaks and imperfections could only have occurred when Charles had tackled Will in the exuberant greeting. Will was without words and without plans as he observed the damage to the vessel that contained me. He remembered the scrolls that foretold of the vessel breaking, whether by fate or fortune, and its contents (me) being swept away into the parallel universe of semi-existence. Will also remembered the promise of transference into another vessel, thereby preventing being swept back into the parallel universe. Will's mind raced as he searched for an appropriate vessel to contain his friend Amir. The mind link was still active and Will beseeched me to help in finding another vessel.

"For my part, I could feel a change within my prison and the formation of a small vortex to one end of the vessel. The vortex was growing and beginning to envelop all that was within its reach. I called out to Will that the vortex was coming nearer and would envelop me, ultimately delivering me into the alternative universe. Will's mind continued to race as he sought an answer to this dilemma and a refuge for his friend. Will's eyes came to focus on the huge English oak he regarded when first he crossed this land. The small box was oak; perhaps the tree of oak would hold Amir and sustain him until his ultimate freedom was attained. Amir was aware of Will's thoughts and agreed to attempt transference to the huge tree.

"Will set out for the tree at a full run just as Amir described the vortex growing larger and more powerful by the second. Will reached the monstrous tree and pulled a dagger from his belt. He used the dagger to strike the trunk of the massive tree in order to dig out a small hole in which he would insert the vessel. The dagger moved quickly, and within moments, a small, square indentation appeared. Will shoved the small box of Palestine oak into the indentation while screaming to me to describe my situation. I shouted back that the vortex had me and I was being inextricably drawn toward the unknown.

"Will's mind reversed to the ancient scrolls and he remembered a passage from Pliny the Elder (father of botany) that most plant life drew sustaining water and minerals through the smallest of roots—even as they drew sunshine through the leaves. Will quickly dug a trench, exposing a tangle of small roots of the massive tree, and placed the tiny, broken box into the ground and next to the smallest roots. Unseen by Will were the microscopic root hairs of the massive oak feeling then penetrating the small oak box. The root hairs multiplied in numbers and penetration sites of the box as I screamed to Will that the vortex was diminishing and another unknown, organic force was drawing me in. Will called and called to me, but his calls were in vain.

"Minutes went by and Will's spirits dropped like the leaves of the oak. One last time, Will called out, 'Commander!' His call was met by silence! Will looked down at the box and was horrified to see that it was rapidly disintegrating before his eyes! Will fell to his knees and reached into the roots to retrieve the box, but it turned to ashes in his hand. Will raised his eyes upward, searching the crown of the oak for any sign of the transference. He saw nothing but a crown of dead leaves still holding on from the winter and ready to be shed. As horror and loss built up within him, Will screamed aloud for Amir Al Braheem, commander of the jinn, but received no reply. His head dropped into his hands and he wept the scalding tears of loss as he had done for his father. The bitter emotions of grief, loss, guilt, remorse, and frustration welled up in Will's throat, making it hard to breathe. Will rose to one knee and then felt a movement underneath him.

"The ground beneath Will began to vibrate. Within seconds, it moved from a vibration to trembling. The trembling then turned into a major tremor. Will was obliged to grasp the trunk of the oak in order not to be sent spinning away. The shaking stopped as suddenly as it had begun, and Will rose to his feet in wonderment. The next thing he heard was a tremendous boom, like a nearby crack of thunder, followed by a rain of last year's leaves and stubborn acorns apparently blown away from their limbs and now falling in a shower to the ground. Within several moments, Will found himself buried to the chest in dead leaves and acorns. At that precise moment, Will's thoughts were filled with my distinctive, baritone voice. *'This Is Good!'*

"Will's brain struggled to contain my thoughts, but he could surmise a joy in me that was unknown until that instant.

"Will called again, 'Commander,' to which I boomed out, 'I am with your thoughts!'

"Will was overjoyed! His tears of loss turned into tears of laughter. Will spoke aloud and he told me of the transfer and how he thought he had lost his friend to the vortex. He told of the loss he felt as the tiny box disintegrated in his hands. I interjected a thought, interrupting Will's tale. My thoughts rang out that I needed no retelling of a story in which I was a player! Will laughed out loud and promised no more repetition.

"He wanted to question me about this new home/vessel/prison, but I interjected another interrupting thought into Will's brain. I told him that I knew he must be curious about this new vessel but that he had not just changed locations for the first time in over two thousand years as I had just done. "I wanted to explore this new domain and how it may affect my preternatural powers over nature. I also thought it best not to reveal what had just happened to anyone! Will understood what it was that I wished to do and could find no reason to object.

"Will offered to go back to the manor house, reveal nothing that had transpired, and return to the big tree in seven days to set plans forward. I agreed, thanked Will for his daring and knowledge of botany, and then closed the mind link. Will's head, however, was still spinning from the recent events, and his mind was filled with questions demanding answers. He brushed away the remaining leaves and acorns to regain his feet. Will gazed upward, into the crown of the tree, but saw no signs of change. He could see the new buds beginning to swell as the weather warmed and the days lengthened. There was no sound emanating from the tree or abnormal atmosphere surrounding the tree. Will turned and began walking back to the manor house. Seven frustrating days lay ahead before his curiosity would be quenched."

Twenty Seven

The Preternatural Oak
The Manor House Grounds, spring 1012

"First, the tree did not seem to 'mind' my presence. That was good! Second, I sensed a huge expansion in my opportunity to engage with this environment. The rigid nature of the huge tree seemed to add structure to me. The height of the tree gave me an ability to engage with the local atmosphere, much more so than when I cleared the channel for Will's passage from Calais. The roots gave me a solid sense of the earth beneath me and a certain control of the grounds surrounding me. Water and minerals entering through the root system came within my control. Not only could these elements reach into, but also I could extend my power through these elements. I did not animate the tree any more than the tree animated me.

"However, as two entities, we did seem to have a symbiosis and more control and power than one of us alone. Lastly, I could access the tree's defensive systems against insects, mold, rot, bacteria, and competitors and receive 'needs' from the tree. Amir could answer these 'needs' by adding or withdrawing energy to and from the tree, much as he had done in helping Sir Robert of Normandy's foal heal. The communication was entirely nonverbal but quite effective.

"At last, the seven days had come and gone. Will headed out to the oak at daybreak. The morning was crisp, and the air was filled with the smoke of hardwoods burning in neighboring fireplaces. The sun rising in the east gave promise of warmth for the day, and the sky was a cloudless blue. Upon reaching the tree, Will closed his eyes and transmitted the familiar entreaty 'Commander,' to which he received the familiar reply 'I am with your thoughts.'

"Will thought of hundreds of questions, but the first ones he asked were to the commander's health, state of consciousness, and sense of his new environment. I remember smiling at my human friend and recent savior. He always seemed to be thinking of others and not himself. I replied that I was very pleased with my new surroundings and that the tree and I were getting along just fine. I continued that I was still exploring new and extended powers that came with this new arrangement but had discovered many new ways to engage with the environment and those within it.

"Instantly, the upper branches of the tree began to move and swirl as if pushed by a strong wind. As Will looked up, the crown of the tree was dipping down toward him and dozens of small branches wrapped around him and swept him upward into the crown. Startled greatly, Will grasped onto a large branch and held on for his life. A great, baritone laugh echoed inside Will's head as I assured him that the commander would not let him fall. The crown bent down again, and other small branches plucked him from his perch and lowered him gently to the ground. It took a moment for Will to resume breathing while his thoughts transmitted that movements like the preceding ones should dissuade potential axmen from molesting the oak!

"Now breathing normally, Will broke out in a long fit of laughter and agreed with me that actions as had just occurred would be a powerful deterrent to anyone wishing to harm the tree. I was pleased that Will was pleased but sensed a reservation in my friend's mind. Will told Amir of his fear, which was if anyone ever witnessed an action such as just happened, they would certainly spread the word of an 'enchanted' tree. Far worse would be if the action that just happened were perceived as evidence of witchcraft or evil possession. Men of good will and evil intent would descend on the grounds in efforts to possess, control, or even destroy the magic within the tree.

"I thought about Will's assessment for a few moments then asked what he would have me do. Will told me that the expansion of my influence over nature was magnificent and worthy of awe. However, in order to protect the tree and even the commander, these powers should be kept secret and employed with discretion and even subterfuge if necessary. The secret was difficult enough to keep when the commander was imprisoned in a small box. This time and in these circumstances, diligence must be our foremost action. Again, I considered Will's words and found them wise. I transmitted thoughts to Will, accepting the proposal and keeping myself and the magic tree unknown to other humans for a while.

"Will said that he would tell his family that the box carrying a small artifact from King Solomon's temple had been damaged and that he had buried it beneath the tree, making it 'hallowed' ground not to be disturbed. I agreed with the plan but also asked Will what it was that he and his family needed right now to further Will's vision of these buildings and lands. Will replied that more than anything in this first year, they needed a good crop to be harvested and the manor house conversion to an inn be completed before winter.

"Amir told Will that he could assist in these outcomes and still remain anonymous. However, I did have another request. When I was imprisoned in the small oak box, I was always at Will's side and could always eavesdrop on his conversations and interactions with others. As Will knew so well, I could also send an interrupting thought into Will's brain, whether or not the mind link was established. Will acknowledged that all these things had happened. I then made his request that Will come out to the tree regularly so that they could communicate with each other. Will also acknowledged that he would greatly miss their regular interaction and would see to it that they would set the mind link often. Both were pleased as Will turned to walk back to the manor house.

"That evening, as the family gathered after dinner to discuss the day's progress, Will told them of burying the relic at the big tree near the manor and that he thought it now should be treated as hallowed. His uncle Charles asked how the ground could be sanctified if there was no priest to say the words. Will said that it was true that he could not sanctify the ground as a priest. However, he could declare that the ground held the ashes of a sanctified relic from the temple of King Solomon and as such should not be disturbed!

"Charles retorted that Will wished to sanctify the grounds and tree as a Druid priest. Had he converted to Druidism in the last few days? Did he wish them all to wear white robes and perform the ritual of the oak and mistletoe? A great laugh emerged from Charles and then all of the aunts and uncles at the thought of young Sir William of Wirral worshipping trees! Will, joining in the joke, added to not forget the gathering of the mistletoe and the boiling in water to make a liquid drink to ward off infertility! Kyrie blushed and the rest of the group howled with laughter. At the end of the merriment, Charles asked Will how they could make the ground 'special.' Will replied that they would build no structure beneath the crown of the tree or let anyone bring harm to the tree with an ax. All agreed!

"As the meeting broke up, Will accompanied Kyrie to the cottage in which he and his father had lived. As they walked and talked of the meeting, their hands brushed each other, then entwined gently. Will told Kyrie of his plans to ask Charles and Donald to step up work on the manor house, particularly the building of apartments for Kyrie and her mother, and kitchen, cupboard, and dining facilities. The long half-day journey from their village to the manor house was tedious and potentially dangerous in inclement weather. He would also build quarters for himself close to the stables to protect them and to advance the breeding and livery businesses.

"Kyrie was happy to hear these things and squeezed Will's hand. He turned toward her and embraced her for several moments. Then he looked into her fierce blue warrior eyes just fast enough to see them close as she brought her lips to his. The earth underneath them trembled for a moment, not enough for them to lose balance but just enough to add significance to the kiss. Kyrie's eyes widened as she looked at Will in amazement. She asked, "Was that an earthquake?" to which Will answered that he did not know. Instantly a thought entered his brain, which he instinctively knew was from me. Will's only interpretation of the thought from me was that it sounded like a giggle followed by 'Remember me!'

Twenty Eight

Fruits of the Labor
Wirral Estates, 1102–1170

"Charles and Donald did step up the renovation of the manor house and completed the apartments for Blinda and Kyrie by the end of summer. Will finished a cottage near the stables and in conjunction with Mathew established blacksmith operations both on the peninsula and the manor house grounds. The weather in 1102 was perfect (if I do say so!) for the farming operations as both Andrew's family and Emma's family reported record crops for harvest. Several severe summer storms seemed to split north and south of the peninsula, doing major damage in central Wales and western Scotland but completely missing the lands and grounds of the Wirral family. Nutrient levels in the farm soil were perfect for the cultivation of every individual crop. Rains versus dry periods could not have been more desirable."

> *Narrator's note: Amir was not quire insufferable here but close. I found it somewhat amusing!*

"Men were hired and overseers were brought on to manage all of the family's holdings, and at the end of the first year, the holding company accounted for a 45 percent profit in assets! Will's idea had worked and worked well. At the end of the year, Will traveled to London to deliver the 10 percent tax to King Edward. The king was happy that all seemed to be working as he and Will had planned. Next year, Edward hoped for the establishment of ports along the River Mersey to increase trade with Ireland and western Scotland. Will promised to begin these projects in AD 1103.

"As the year drew to a close and Will was completely assured that all was operating well, he escorted Kyrie into the night, and in the presence of my tree, he asked Kyrie to be his wife and partner under a full moon and starlit sky. For an educated man, Will stumbled for the right words to convey his love and desire for Kyrie.

"All that he tried to say seemed trite and lacking in conviction until my voice echoed in his head, 'Valkyrie, I have loved you since the day we met at the massive oak and you threatened to shoot me with that English longbow. A year has passed since that first encounter, and I find my love and respect for you growing as wheat in the fields. If you were to consent to be my wife and partner for the balance of our lifetimes, I would promise to love, protect, cherish, and honor you until the day that I die.'

"Will swallowed hard, trying to remember the exact words from Amir, and then, dropping to one knee and holding her hands, he recited the words as if they were his own, because in reality, they were his own. Kyrie drew Will from his knee and, looking into his eyes, said, 'Sir William of Wirral, I have loved you since the day we met at the massive oak and I feigned to shoot you with the longbow. A year has passed, and since that first encounter, I find my love and respect for you growing as wheat in the fields. I do consent to be your wife and partner for the balance of our lifetimes, and I do promise to love, protect, cherish, and honor you until the day that I die.'

"At that instant, the earth trembled for a few moments, not enough for the couple to lose balance but enough to add emphasis to the proposals. As Will and Kyrie embraced and kissed in the moonlight to seal their pact, a thought from me entered Will's brain. 'Nicely done, and you may thank me later.'

"Will and Kyrie were married at the summer solstice with all of the Wirral clan in attendance. The workers and overseers of the family were invited, and a great feast was prepared with aunts Laura, Ann, and Emma in charge of the food preparation. Lamb, beef, and pheasants were presented along with fresh breads and berries from the forest. Charles hauled an oxcart laden with jars of wine along with several combs of wild honey. Musicians from nearby Chester played the lute and lyre, and even King Edward sent an emissary bearing gifts for the newlyweds.

"As the celebration continued into the night, Will and Kyrie stole away to the small cottage near the stables. Kyrie's mother Blinda had decorated the home with fresh mistletoe and scented candles. Wine and water were placed in jars on the table along with bread and cheeses from the feast. Will and Kyrie held each other as if some force were trying to tear them apart. They kissed as if this were the only kiss. Tomorrow, they would emerge and go back to work as spouses and partners, their entire lives spread out before them. Responsibilities, schedules, and toil lay ahead. But tonight was theirs and theirs alone. Almost! One last thought entered Will's head as he doused the candles for the night. 'You have done well. Please remember me.'

"Will and Kyrie's life was filled with joy, success, and four sons! The manor house became known as Kyrie's Inn and was heralded far and wide as having excellent rooms and the finest of foods for travelers. The shops and businesses flourished as the inn's reputation grew. Will and Kyrie were successful in breeding a large herd of the Arabians, which were always in high demand. Charles, who married Blinda later that same year, and Donald, working with local boatwrights and dock builders, established working ports on the River Mersey servicing the growing town of Liverpool, west Scotland, Ireland, and southwest Britain. During this time, all enjoyed the fairest of weather and most suitable farming conditions.

Storms coming across from Ireland continued to split apart before crossing into Wirral. Serious disease and sickness also avoided the peninsula, leaving some to wonder if the peninsula was enchanted.

"Of all Will's ventures, the dearest to his heart was setting up a series of schools. Education was always a gift to the nobles and gentry of the land. Commoners and serfs rarely had the opportunity of any education except what could be learned at home or from neighbors. The schools were free to the students, requiring only the permission of the parent and any nobleman who may have some power over the child's time. Will never experienced any rejection from a parent or noble for any child who wished to go to school. The schools were financed by the Wirral Holding Company, which had grown into one of Britain's largest groups of merchants, warehousemen, shopkeepers, horse breeders, vintners, and woodsmen.

"All students were taught Latin along with the math and sciences of the ancients. Vocational classes and apprenticeships were available to prepare those students showing promise as skilled tradesmen. Many of the Wirral extended family taught at these schools, and if some students showed great promise in the classics, they could receive introduction to a university such as Oxford.

"Will, Kyrie, and their four sons lived a full and happy life. The businesses continued to flourish, Will's herd of Arabians was the finest in Britain, and he was called upon regularly to train and deliver an Arabian to a new knight or lady. Will and Kyrie aged gracefully and without the burdens of debt or sickness. Their sons grew strong and capable, finding wives and starting their own journeys through life. Will continued to visit and talk to his old friend. For my part, although not completely free, I enjoyed my interaction with this group of humans.

"I noted the physical changes that time brought to humans and did not understand how they could embrace their mortality and eventual death, something I would never face. My friend Will's blond hair had turned white, and some of the fierceness of his blue eyes had faded. Unknown to Will, I had intervened several times in his life to alter a potential serious illness. Diseases of the joints, heart, and viscera that had appeared within Will were quickly dispatched by me without Will's knowledge. I knew that at some time I must let my friend go. But I would not do so yet!

"Years passed, and as they did, the generation of Wirrals that included Will's father, Richard—Charles, Donald, Andrew, Emma, Ann, and Laura—lived into their eighties and passed away in their time. Blinda died the year after Charles passed away, and all business moved to their heirs. The enterprises continued to be profitable, and the extended family grew and branched out into new endeavors. Will was pleased that all had gone so well and that his uncles and aunts had lived full and prosperous lives. His generation was beginning to turn businesses over to grandchildren, and life moved on inexorably. At all times, I kept watch and kept quiet, assisting the family as I could and protecting them from harm. I was not free but I was powerful and I was needed. Freedom would come someday."

> *Narrator's note: At the end of this session, Amir inquired as to the results of the medical scans I had completed. I told him that I had not heard from the hospital and did not know what the results would have in store for me. For the first time in all the weeks of our interactions, he reached out and placed his hand on my shoulder. "Start to dream of your future, my friend!" It would be several weeks before I understood his message.*

The Death of Sir William
The Kyrie Inn, summer 1163

"On an early summer's eve in AD 1163, Will and Kyrie had their dinner and walked outside of the inn to enjoy the warm evening. Kyrie spoke of their good fortune and wonderful life they had shared. Will was approaching his eightieth birthday and walked slowly and deliberately with Kyrie on one arm. Her touch still thrilled him, and he never wanted to let her go. She spoke of their sons and daughters-in-law with families of their own and how proud she was of them all. She then turned to Will and told him that even with the entire family's help, it had been him, Will, who was the architect of it all. He was the one with the wisdom and vision that had set the course for all of their success. Will remarked that he may have been the catalyst but it took everyone's labor and persistence to succeed.

"They stood there in the dark and looked up at the black sky shimmering with stars and planets. They embraced for a long moment and returned to their apartment in the inn. As they lay next to each other, Kyrie leaned over to kiss Will good night. The kiss was soft and warm and full of a lifetime of love. Will returned her kiss and, wishing her a good night, fell immediately asleep. Kyrie turned toward him and grasped his hand. Her eyelids fluttered twice and she took a deep, long, last breath.

"The next morning, Will was sitting outside his cottage, staring up at the sky, when a familiar voice echoed in his head. 'Will?' Will answered, 'Commander.' My thoughts now began to pour into Will's brain. I could not find Kyrie's thoughts. Had she left on a trip? What was the emptiness I sensed in Will this day? What could I do? Will answered me slowly that she was gone. She had passed away during the night. Will told me of waking early in the morning to find Kyrie clutching his hand and with unblinking eyes looking at his face. Will described a look of peace and contentment on her face as he rose up to awaken her to no avail. He felt around her neck for the pulse of her heart and found none. Will described that with all his knowledge he could not bring her back to him. Large, hot tears were streaming down Will's face as he asked me how he could survive without her. The hole in his chest was too big for anything to fill, and he wished he would have died with her.

"Will's thoughts and emotions were so powerful in their sadness, anxiety, and sense of loss that I was unable to communicate. When I finally did, I asked Will to return to his bedside and let me see Kyrie through his eyes. Will lifted himself up shakily and went inside the cottage where Kyrie lay. I stared through Will's eyes and observed all that he had told me. I told Will that I had not foreseen this and that I was saddened and ashamed that I had not been able to intervene. I told Will that I had no power to animate a human. Those powers were reserved to only One. I continued that I did possess the powers of the ancient pharaohs of Egypt and could preserve her body in death for thousands of years if that is what Will wished. Will was not ready to let her go so he agreed and asked if she could be buried underneath the massive oak where they had first met. I said that I would be honored and would protect her grave even unto my own annihilation.

"The days passed and everyone in the extended family gathered for the burial. Some wondered why Kyrie was being laid to rest here instead of the family cemetery, but no one objected to Will's instructions. Some words were spoken and flowers were laid on the rendered earth, then all departed to their home. Inside of the wooden coffin, I had transformed Kyrie's simple burial clothes to the richest silk gown. Her hair was returned to its original blonde, and a tiara of preserved flowers adorned her head. I arranged her arms and folded her hands in a position of repose and finally placed an invisible cover over her body—rich with rare earths and oils to preserve her as she was now for a thousand years. I transmitted this thought to Will and watched as he wept again.

"Two weeks later, his sons found Will lying across Kyrie's gravesite. He was clutching a scroll with what looked to be writings in Egyptian. He had died that night as he visited her grave. As with their mother, Will's sons found a look of peace and fulfillment on his face. They decided to lay their father beside their mother at the oak tree. The family gathered as they had two weeks earlier with lots of talk about the greatness of William in business and his inability to live without Kyrie. Since no one could translate the scroll, the sons decided to bury it with their father. Words were spoken and flowers were laid upon the grounds, then all departed to their homes.

"I made the same arrangements with Will's body and dressed him in lavish robes, preserving his body and placing the scroll in his folded hands. Days later, one of the sons passed by the tree and discovered a strange phenomenon: sap dripping from every leaf in the oak's crown. His son described this to the family as the tree 'crying,' and all were amazed.

"I was devastated. As an immortal, I would never face death, but death would affect me by taking away any humans I might befriend or endeavor to help. In addition, who would help me gain my freedom now? I did not think after all my travels and deeds that this tree was my ultimate destiny. I could look at Will's preserved body and remember their times together, but I would never hear Will calling out, 'Commander!'

"In all the preparations, I did not read the scroll that was buried with Will. I saw the words in the ancient Egyptian language with which I was very familiar and was curious as to its contents. Curiosity finally overwhelmed my grief and my thoughts entered the coffin and began reading the scroll.

"Commander and dear friend, my only regret in this life was not being able to help you attain your ultimate freedom. I do not believe that existence in this tree, as wonderful as it is, can be your ultimate destiny. I do believe you will be tested in the future. How and by what/whom you will be tested is not in my thoughts. I do feel in the deepest fabric of my being that you will pass that test and become free. Until that time, I ask you to protect our family and allow them to prosper. In your wisdom, you will know what actions are required. Think of me as I will think of you and 'I will remember you always.'"

> *Narrator's note: Immediately upon finishing the last sentence in this session, Amir vanished. I can only conjecture that the telling of this part of his story filled him with great pain, even after one thousand years had passed.*

Thirty

The Great Pestilence
The Wirral Peninsula, summer 1349

"Something was coming! Something was coming from China. It traveled along well-established trade routes overland and by sea. It was a killer that would decimate over one half of the population of Europe before it would go away, only to return in later years. In some locations, it would kill over three quarters of the inhabitants of a village. It had no respect for rank or privilege, king or slave. There was no treatment, and there was no cure, although healers of the time tried the time-tested cures and remedies of the past. It could not be seen, although it appeared to be carried by rats. Wherever rats were few, the evil was scarce. If you were afflicted, your chance of survival was one in two. If you were old or young, your chance of survival was one in five. If you were already sick with any other malady, your chance of survival was zero!

"It starts out with you feeling poor, listless, achy, and feverish. As the evil progresses, your lymph nodes would swell into masses called buboes. After two or three days, the buboes would rupture and turn black, spilling the evil into your blood where it invaded the kidneys, brain, and spleen. The blood would carry it to all parts of the body, overwhelming the immune system. Bleeding would occur from the mouth, ears, and nose as gangrenous limbs began to decompose even before death. Mercifully, death followed quickly in a matter of days or, if particularly nasty, up to two weeks. As it passed through Europe this first time, it was known as 'the Great Pestilence' and 'the Great Mortality.' Three hundred years later, it would be referred to as 'the Black Death.'"

Amir had sensed, even heard about, this coming crisis but being held in place by the oak limited his range of reception. Then there were the stories told by merchants and tradesmen who had traveled to the European continent of a sickness sweeping across the Bosporus and into Greece. Once on the continent, it marched steadily into central Europe, Italy, Spain, and France. It would only be a matter of time before it arrived on the island of Britain.

"In the six generations of Wirrals who lived here since the death of Will and Kyrie, times had been favorable. Mild weather and good growing conditions had helped the Wirral agricultural holdings grow considerably. Food and grains were now exported throughout England, and with the working ports, established by the founding generation of Wirrals, exports also were traveling to Scotland, Ireland, and some Scandinavian countries. The old manor house, Kyrie Inn, had been rebuilt and doubled in size to meet the demand of travelers. The herd of Arabian horses was always in high demand, sometimes outstripping the supply and leading to premium prices.

"I would quietly intervene on occasion to assist the heirs of Will and his family but generally remained aloof and silent. I never befriended another human like I did Will. I would place a thought into the brain of someone on occasion, but it would appear as an idea, not a conversation. I never forgot Will's message on the scroll regarding his ultimate destiny and waited patiently for the time when he would be released from the tree. For me, a few hundred years was meaningless and I would wait. However, I was troubled by this approaching plague and sharpened my senses for any news of its arrival here.

"In later years, historians would debate just how and when

the Great Pestilence arrived in England, but most would assert it arrived in the summer of 1348. By summer of 1349, it had traversed the entire island, decimating the populations of cities, towns, and villages. It would later be known that the plague was transmitted by the bite of an infected flea, drawing the evil from rats that acted as a reservoir for the infecting agent. In the fall, the first humans to become afflicted among the Wirral extended family were four stable workers. The overseer went to their cottages when they did not show up for work and found them ill with a fever and general malaise. Within two days, the tell-tale buboes appeared on the workers and their situation worsened. Four days later, three were dead and the fourth was struggling for his life.

"Within a week of this first outbreak, the sickness was affecting nearly three quarters of the extended family and people who worked for the family with death rates approaching one in two. I could do little to intervene on such a massive scale and was exceedingly frustrated at this lack of ability. If I could touch an infected person, I may be able to help as I had done with Will's ailments. But this physical contact was unlikely since the disease was ruling everyday actions. Most were sick and the rest cared for the sick, ruling out anyone coming within reach of the tree.

"And then it happened. I became aware of a female child of about ten years stumbling toward the massive oak. The child fell and vomited violently before struggling to her feet. She was moaning feebly, pale, and in obvious distress. I sensed the formation of buboes on the child and that they were turning black. The child would die a horrible death in a matter of days. I sent a thought into her feverish brain, telling her to come near to the big tree. The child's head snapped to the right as her perception of my thought registered in her head. The child called out, 'Is this Mother's spirit calling?' I realized instantly that her mother must be dead. I called out to her again, telling her that I was a jinn—er, spirit of the tree and that I could help her feel better. The child called back, asking if the spirit was evil and meant to scare her. In my most soothing fashion, I placed a picture of a most sublime being, wishing to help, and again asked her to come near to the tree. She stumbled forward on unsteady feet toward the tree and me, hesitating slightly. I cooed in her head and told her, 'Come on, little one.'

"Two more steps, and she was there. She heard a rustle in the leaves above her as if a great wind was upon her, followed by the touch of many small branches wrapping around her and pulling her upward into the crown. The child whimpered slightly, but I reassured her that I was a good spirit and would help her. The child relaxed as I peered into the depths of a bubo where I saw countless organisms multiplying and spreading from there and invading her organs.

"I concentrated on providing the powerful energy of the jinn into her body and at the same time withdrawing energy from the organisms. I had never attempted this before but was careful in my intervention so as not to overwhelm the small and desperately sick body. In a few moments, the child's eyes fluttered and opened. A small scream issued from her mouth as she found herself sixty feet off the ground, entwined by tree branches. Another soothing thought, and she relaxed again. Unknown to her, the incoming flow of energy caused her immune system to engage fiercely, and the withdrawal of energy from the invading organisms was causing them to break apart. The child called out that she was feeling better but was afraid of heights. I gently lowered her to the ground but said that she must hold onto the tree trunk for a few more moments. The moments passed and Amir told the little girl that she could let go of the trunk and that she would continue feeling better. She smiled faintly then slipped to the ground and fell asleep immediately. The shock on her body had taken what reserves she had left and exhaustion had won out. Oddly, I felt a wave of exhaustion pass over me. It faded quickly and I gave it no further thought. I placed one more thought into the child's mind as she slept. 'Remember me.'"

Thirty One

Reconciliation
The Big Oak, fall 1349

"The next morning, the child awoke shivering in wet clothes due to the morning's chill. Her fever had broken and she had sweated profusely during the night. Except for shivering and her teeth chattering, she felt good. Her face had lost the pall of death and color had returned. She felt exhausted but well! Somewhere in the back of her mind, she knew she was supposed to remember someone for helping her. Had she dreamed the events of last night about a spirit in the tree, talking to her and making her well? I linked into her thoughts and said, 'It was no dream.' The child's hands went to her head, feeling that something was in her mind. I told her not to worry and that I was the spirit in the tree who had cured her. Her head spun wildly, looking for the source of the voice in her head.

"I asked her if she remembered being taken up high into the tree, and she did. Seeing her still shivering, I asked if she would like to warm up. She answered yes, and I told her to put her hand on the trunk of the tree. She hesitated, but I explained to her it was like a magic trick and would be fun. She touched the tree, and instantly her clothes were dry and she was toasty warm as if she had been wrapped in blankets.

"The child backed up a few steps, looked up at the tree, and said, 'You are the one I am supposed to remember, aren't you?' I told her it was me that had helped cure her yesterday. I told her that I had been helping the Wirral clan for hundreds of years and that an ancestor of hers had been a dear friend long ago. I asked her name, and the child said her name was Valkyrie but everyone just called her Val. I laughed gently and told her I once knew a young woman named Valkyrie. But everyone called her Kyrie. She was tall and beautiful as I thought Val would be. She snickered and blushed at the compliment.

"I told Val that shc had important work to do. I could help all the people in her village and the inn, but I must see and survey the size of the task that lay before me. I said to Val that I could see through her memories but wanted her to understand what would happen. She was reluctant and asked me if this thing I wanted to do would hurt. I assured her that it would not hurt, but as he looked through her memories, she would be able to look through his mind as well. He told her not to be scared but to be brave and help him help her family.

"Val asked what she had to do, and I told her to relax, close her eyes, and be brave. At once, he was linked to her mind and her most overwhelming memories were of her family, the plague, and her mother. Through her memories, I witnessed the agony and despair as man lost wife, mother lost child, and children lost entire family groups. I would never know death like these humans would as a normal part of life. But this was not normal. This disease was inexorable and hideous, leaving nothing behind but death and the agony of loss. It was no way for anyone to die, and I would use my powers to eradicate this pestilence—at least from this small part of the world.

"I moved out of Val's mind and asked her if she was well. Val looked at the huge tree and told me that she knew what I was. Val told me that she saw a creature about twenty feet tall and having no hair. She continued that she saw a man and woman in shining robes that I kept close in my memories. She told me that I was also sad because I could not leave the tree. I said that she was very observant and wise for her age, at which she snickered and blushed again.

"I said to her, 'Tell me, little one, if I am imprisoned in this tree, how do I travel to where my powers are needed?' Val thought for a moment, gazing up into the tree, and said, 'Put your magic into the acorns, and I will take them to my family to help them. The tree cannot move, but the acorns move a lot. They fall and roll away, squirrels carry them away, and some boys in the village even throw them at me. By whatever means, the acorns are moved to different places.' I was speechless, which was unusual in and of itself. It was simple yet elegant. Could it work?

"I would attempt it with all my powers. I told Val to run back to her village and find people who were not afflicted and have them bring vessels to carry the acorns back to the sick. Val asked what he would be doing while she was gone. Amir said that he would be preparing the acorns. Val asked what to do if no one believed her. Amir calmed her mind and told her that all would believe her by just looking at her, cured as she is now. Lastly, he told her when she returned to gather as many acorns as she and the others could carry, take them back, and put several in the hands of all who were afflicted. They must hold them close to their chest for at least several minutes. Val nodded in agreement, turned, and ran toward the village.

"There were literally thousands of acorns on the massive oak, and to be effective, each one would have to hold a certain amount of healing energy—both to energize the immune system and to destroy the offending organisms. Since the oak had held my energy without harm to itself, the acorns of the big tree might be as strong. I had never attempted to transfer as much of the energy that composed my actual being, outside of himself. I was cognizant that when even small amounts of energy were used, he would be aware of a slight dip in my composition. This was never worrisome because I could recharge myself quickly from the elements in the earth and atmosphere.

"However, this time would be different. I did not fear death but was conscious that I might extinguish myself passed my ability to recover. No matter. I would not stand by and witness everything that Will, Kyrie, and their families had built be destroyed by this unseen organism. I concentrated the flow of energy to the crown and acorns of the big tree and unleashed a mighty blast from my outstretched hands.

"Instantly, the crown of the tree began to shine in a low and pulsing glow. The glow began to grow and change colors from dull orange to bright red and finally to a blinding white. Sparks and rays of light shot out from the crown and showered the ground below. My instinct for self-preservation was screaming for me to cease the flow, but I unleashed a second blast of energy toward the crown. The ground beneath the tree began to shake violently and the crown appeared to explode, creating a tremendous sound like a lightning strike in a storm. Thousands of glowing acorns hurtled toward the ground in waves like sheets of wooden rain. They struck the earth sounding similar to hail, and the thousands of strikes blended into a drumroll of projectiles. On the ground, the glowing projectiles pulsed with color, seeming to cool from the blinding white to red, orange, and finally the shiny brown born by most acorns. And then there was silence!

"Val and about three dozen of her friends and relatives returned to the tree while carrying sacks and baskets to gather the acorns. All had been amazed at Val's condition and apparent cure from this dreaded disease. Few required much coaxing to return with her as directed by the spirit in the tree. They immediately set about gathering as many acorns as they could carry. All would remark on how hot the acorns seemed to be, as if drawn from an oven. Hot or not, Val's friends and family gathered every acorn they could find and started back to the village to treat the afflicted. Val carried a sack full of hope for her family. Then she turned back toward the silent tree and called out to the spirit. Her calls were met with silence, and she moved away toward home.

"As a being composed of energy, my energy was that of ten thousand men. But now, my energy was that of a single candle. I had come perilously close to extinguishing himself. I was too weak to speak when Val called to him. I was too weak to even place a simple thought into her mind. Would I ever know if my energy had done anything to check the dreadful disease? I could not feel myself regenerating and wondered what my destiny might have been. Suddenly, in the midst of this depression, an image began to form in my mind. The image grew lighter and clearer until I could see the shapes of two humans—male and female. I wondered if I was having hallucinations in this weakened state. As the images moved into clear focus, Amir heard a voice from the past calling out to him, 'Commander!'

"To which I answered, 'I am with your thoughts.'

"The image and the voice were of Will. Kyrie stood beside him, and they were surrounded by the purest of white light. She smiled at Amir as Will continued. I asked to look through Will's eyes at the village of Val. Instantly, another vision of the sickest people rising from their beds, smiling, and embracing each other with tears in their eyes and acorns in their hand. I was as joyous as I could be in this weakened state. I told Will that it was the little girl, Val, who had the idea to transfer my energy to the acorns and that I was proud of her courage and bravery. Will told me that Val was a sixth-generation grandchild and that he too was proud. The image of Will and Kyrie began to waver and fade. I begged (which I had never done) for Will and Kyrie to stay with me. Or if it was the Most High's wish, let him become mortal to die and to have the chance of living eternally with his friend.

"Will's image sharpened, and he told me that I was reconciled to the Most High and had earned the destiny of watching and intervening on mankind's behalf for the rest of the age. My judgment had been proven worthy and just, and his freedom and free will were now restored. I was about to give thanks when Will said in a commanding voice, 'Now prepare yourself!'

"A single streak of blue-white lightning appeared in a cloudless sky. It seemed to hover, thousands of feet in the air, for a few seconds before descending to earth and striking the tree in the trunk. The tree and ground around it shook violently, and a deafening report of thunder rumbled on for what seemed like minutes. The massive tree trunk split in two from the lowest branch to the upper roots. I arose from the tree, all twenty feet of me, now glistening with new energy. I stooped down to gather a huge fistful of acorns. 'Powerful acorns will make powerful trees!' I roared. Then I looked skyward as my image lengthened into a thin bolt of smokeless fire and shot upward into the heavens, arching over Val's village and heading westward toward Ireland, the Atlantic Ocean, and the unknown.

"Val and her family looked up as I passed over, and they marveled at lightning on a clear day. But Val had a different idea, and she told her family that she believed the spirit in the tree was off to help other people. She received no argument from child or adult. Then she exclaimed that there were thousands of acorns left and that they should split up and take the cure to the surrounding areas.

"After many days of travel and curing the vile pestilence, Val returned to her village and went out to see the big tree. Amazingly, the tree was not dead from the lightning strike. It seemed to have been cauterized at the split to form two trees. She started to move closer when she noticed a small box on the ground. She went to pick it up and a thought popped into her mind. 'I carved this box from the trunk of the big tree. A part of me is inside, and you may call on me in times of need or trouble. Do not waste its power, little one. Remember me!' Val walked over to the tree and hugged the trunks one last time, took the small box, and departed for home.

Narrator's note: I assumed that this story was concluded and switched off my cassette recorder when Amir directed me to the several acorns in the box with his other mementos. He told me that these acorns were gathered up by him when he was freed from his tree prison back in England. He said that he had planted most of them and that these few were all that remained. He handed the acorns over to me, and an instant warmth was evident. After several moments, he took the acorns from my hand and said I should have my medical scans rechecked. He also told me that the acorns produced many trees, some in this area. He glanced at the cassette recorder and commented that the cassette was full.

"That is enough for tonight," he said gently.

Then he told me there were more stories he wished to tell and have recorded. He wished me a pleasant evening and vanished from the room. The warmth I felt from the acorns was spreading from my hand up my arm, across my chest, up to my face, and into my abdomen. As the warmth enveloped me, I felt a calm and sense of well-being I had not felt in over a year.

"I think I'll call my oncologist tomorrow and ask him to run the scans again.

The faint sound of a voice rose above the crash of the waves.

"Remember me!"

EPILOGUE

Friend of the Family
Brunswick County, North Carolina, 2919

Narrator's note:

One crisp, fall evening, Amir appeared on my front porch as I was sipping a Jack Daniel's in my rocker and contemplating the stars in the constellation Orion. He seemed relaxed and in good spirits, which was not always the case.

"May I sit?" he asked.

Now this was totally out of character! Amir, the last of the jinn, commanded. He did not ask permission!

"Please join me," I answered as my eyebrows arched in disbelief.

"I have another tale I wish to record and have you transcribe. Do you feel up to it tonight?"

"The evening is beautiful and the stars are magnificent. Shall I bring my recorder to the porch and record out here?

"That would be acceptable." He grinned as the cassette recorder appeared on the porch table beside me and switched itself on. He began to speak as a storyteller would, skillfully weaving the tale.

And there it was!

It was at least ninety feet at the crown and better than a one-hundred-foot spread. He stopped the Honda Pilot and just marveled at the thing! As William Franklin Wirral, PhD, got out of the car on that early November day, both knees sent sharp reminders as to the state of degeneration within the joint capsules. They would relent as he moved around more and got them going. The morning air was crisp but promising warmth. Such was the weather on the South Brunswick Islands of North Carolina. Autumn at the beach was his favorite time. Gone were the mosquitos, tourists, and humidity, but that cloudless, "Carolina Blue" sky still covered the heavens. North Carolina was his home state—where he was born, raised, educated, and married. For the last forty years, Dr. Wirral had been involved in family, children, graduate school, and a career in clinical research that required twelve moves and twelve real estate closings. Shreveport, Louisiana; Philadelphia (twice); Chicago; Austin, Texas; Nutley, New Jersey; and Palo Alto, California, were among the places they called home.

His wife and kids must have been nomadic in another life because all seemed to thrive with every move. Kate, his wife of forty-four years, would question every move but always support the arguments about this move being the best thing for them. But there was no argument that they would retire on the North Carolina coast.

He had worked at some job or other since age ten. Now, suddenly at sixty-five, he had nothing to do. He didn't play golf, bridge, or board games. He read but needed a rest for the eyes every once in a while. So one day when he was pestering Kate about being bored, she asked about reviving his love of plants into some kind of hobby or activity. She reminded him about the impromptu lectures given in the car as they drove to vacation sites at the mountains or coast. Didn't she recall a special interest surrounding large, specimen trees? Didn't she remember that he would go on and on about some giant, famous tree and the role it played in somebody's history? Treaty Oak? Seven Sisters Oak? Emancipation Oak? Jackson's Big Oak BBQ Oak? Saint Simons Island Oak? The *USS Constitution's* oak structural side ribs?

It struck him!

> *Narrator's note: Although he never admitted it, here is where I believe Amir intervened.*

What if he took a couple of weeks to find and photograph some of the better-known giant oaks? Live oaks were extraordinary in size, girth, and age! *Quercus virginianum* covered in Spanish moss, gnarly in branch formation, and hardened by storms—almost magical!

There surely was something magical about this specimen. The tree was near the town of Ocean Isle Beach, North Carolina, a popular summer vacation spot and now his retirement home. His grandkids (Liz, who was fifteen, and Joe, who was eleven) were down from Wilmington for the weekend and already had poles, bait, and a spot picked out for some back-creek fishing. Flounder this time. Both were great kids. Wirral thought that whoever said that being a grandparent was a reward from God had it right.

Joe was outgrowing trousers at an alarming rate. He was smart, athletic, and a future ladies' man for sure. Liz was already taller than her mother and still growing. At five feet, eight inches, she was approaching statuesque! Her straight blonde hair reached down to her waist, and her eyes were the color of a deep, still lake. Both had been extraordinarily healthy, suffering few childhood maladies until three years ago. Liz seemed to lose color, strength, and appetite in less than a week.

It took several trips to FPs, IMs, and finally a hematologist to uncover the cause. Wirral knew he had to be back home in time to get her to New Hanover Regional Hospital in Wilmington. Next to Duke University, New Hanover had one of the best oncology units in the state. Liz had been successfully fighting acute lymphocytic leukemia for three years. Her last blood tests were not as good as her oncologist wanted them, and there was a slight fear that she might be coming out of remission. She had been a little pale and tired but was not going to miss the flounder trip. She promised to meet him back home at 2 p.m. for the forty-five-minute trip up to Wilmington. It was just a recheck of the blood values and they would be back home in plenty of time to fry that flounder. Joe wanted to go with them too but only if he got to ride shotgun in the Pilot!

Wirral drove west on NC 179 out of Shallotte about four miles to Piggott Road, turned left and drove two miles, and then turned right onto Village Point Road. Three hundred yards toward Inlet Point Restaurant, and there it was. "God, it's a big sucker!" he mused. A hand-painted sign hanging from a low branch said the tree was over two thousand years old. That might be a stretch, he thought, but he would bet two Mountain Dews and a MoonPie that that tree was here 1,200–1,500 years ago. Strangely, he had seen hundreds of these oaks, some as big as or bigger than this one. What was it that made him feel the tree was something more than a big oak? Something almost magical!

He took about twenty pictures from multiple angles and was successful in getting other objects in the shots to give the tree some scale and photographic evidence of its enormity. Before leaving, he picked up a handful of acorns that had landed near the Pilot and shoved them into his pants pocket. He had always marveled that such a small acorn (other oaks had much larger acorns) could produce such a mammoth tree! He climbed back into the Pilot, fully expecting another reminder from his knees.

"Damn! That wasn't bad!" he exclaimed. Moving around always loosened them up. As he headed back toward home, the day's promise of warmth was being fulfilled.

The old man pulled the Pilot into the driveway back at the house at exactly 2 p.m. to find Liz and Joe waiting on the porch. Shouts of greeting and hugs all around, they climbed back into the Pilot with Joe riding shotgun as promised and headed out to Wilmington, the hospital, and a verdict. Liz situated her long frame into the back seat behind Joe and plugged her iPhone into the truck's power plug. She was definitely not as full of energy as usual and not as talkative. Joe was going on about his next merit badge in Boy Scouts and how he might ask for help while studying the swamp outside Shallotte. Wirral said of course he would help and glanced into the rearview mirror at Liz. She was sending texts at a hypersonic speed, which was quite an accomplishment since she was typing with two fingers and a thumb!

By the time they got to US-17, Joe was onto his latest achievement with *Minecraft*. There were no sounds coming from the back seat. Wirral glanced again into the rearview mirror and Liz was still on the iPhone, texting away. He asked her why she was so quiet but only got a muffled response. He asked again more pointedly if she was all right, and she said she was OK, just tired. He asked her if he should pull over or find a Hardee's and get her a Coke.

She replied, "No, thank you."

Then he asked if this upcoming blood test was bothering her. Bingo! Liz burst into tears and put her face in her hands. Words started spilling out, and it was obvious that she was terrified the cancer was coming back and fearful of potential radiation and chemo and maybe even bone marrow transplants. He pulled the Pilot over to the breakdown lane and turned to face her. He said that it was OK to be scared. Anyone who was not scared of cancer was obviously "three bricks shy of a load." That remark always made her giggle, and it did not fail this time. He quickly changed the subject now that she had relaxed a little and told her about the huge live oak he had found and photographed and asked if she and Joe would like to go see it on the way home. All agreed that was an excellent idea, and to punctuate the decision, he reached into his pocket and produced the handful of acorns that had been collected from the tree. He divided them up and gave half to Liz and half to Joe, but for some unknown reason, Joe passed his acorns over to Liz. Her next comment was that the acorns were almost hot.

"Did you heat them up or something?" she asked.

He replied that they had been in his pocket and in the Pilot for an hour so maybe they warmed up when he ran the heater a little earlier. The explanation seemed acceptable to both, and Liz slipped them into her pocket.

Unknown to all occupants of the Pilot, subcellular and molecular changes began occurring within Liz's body. A genetic mutation in the PAX5 regulatory gene reversed its faulty transcription, as did other genes involved with her cancer. A sudden rush of killer T cells flooded her circulatory system, and new noncancerous phagocytes began attacking and destroying the cancerous white cells of leukemia.

They got back on the road and the mood seemed lifted. Wirral remarked to Liz that the blood test was screening for only one factor and that her parents would probably have the results by morning. Liz said that suited her fine, and she was anxious to get back to flounder fishing.

They pulled up to the outpatient entrance at New Hanover Memorial, and Liz took off alone toward a waiting nurse.

Within minutes, she returned and they were on their way home. Liz seemed to have regained some of her color, and she had definitely regained her voice, talking almost nonstop the entire way home. With all his calm and common sense advice to Liz, he was still terrified that the blood test would reveal bad news. And then the strangest thing occurred. A random thought, almost a shout, popped into his head from out of nowhere.

"She will be well. Consider this a gift from a friend of the family."

Narrator's note: I met Dr. Wirral during one of my walks on the beach. We became casual friends—beach-walking buddies, I guess. On one such walk, I asked about his ancestry, and he told me that he traced his family name back to England and the Crusades. Coincidence? I think not.

I did have my medical scans rechecked and was and continue to be cancer-free. I also continue to transcribe for Amir on occasion when he has a story to share.